A ROSE FOR MAMA
By Flo Maxwell

© Copyright 2006 Florine Maxwell
All rights reserved. No part of this publication may be reproduced, stored in a retrieval system, or transmitted, in any form or by any means, electronic, mechanical, photocopying, recording, or otherwise, without the written prior permission of the author.

Note for Librarians: A cataloguing record for this book is available from Library and Archives Canada at www.collectionscanada.ca/amicus/index-e.html
ISBN 1-4120-8917-4

Printed in Victoria, BC, Canada. Printed on paper with minimum 30% recycled fibre. Trafford's print shop runs on "green energy" from solar, wind and other environmentally-friendly power sources.

Offices in Canada, USA, Ireland and UK

Book sales for North America and international:
Trafford Publishing, 6E–2333 Government St.,
Victoria, BC V8T 4P4 CANADA
phone 250 383 6864 (toll-free 1 888 232 4444)
fax 250 383 6804; email to orders@trafford.com

Book sales in Europe:
Trafford Publishing (UK) Limited, 9 Park End Street, 2nd Floor
Oxford, UK OX1 1HH UNITED KINGDOM
phone +44 (0)1865 722 113 (local rate 0845 230 9601)
facsimile +44 (0)1865 722 868; info.uk@trafford.com

Order online at:
trafford.com/06-0673

10 9 8 7 6 5 4 3

DEDICATION

Especially to my three children, Kenneth and Tina Spann and Michael Maxwell. The day that I heard Shirley Caesar's Recordings of "No Charge" and "Don't Drive Your Mama Away" I thought about my own children and realized that, "But for the Grace of God that could be me."

I used my children, two boys and a girl in the middle, as a template and let my imagination run free; hence, this fictionalized novel.

To the Holy Spirit. He has been my Teacher, my Guide, my Helper and my Best Friend.

ACKNOWLEDGMENT

I feel obliged to acknowledge the songs which have been incorporated into this book along with the artists who recorded them where possible. They have been a blessing to me through the years.

SHIRLEY CAESAR,
"No Charge"
"He'll Do It Again"
"Don't Drive Your Mama Away"
"How Long Has It Been Since You Been Home?"
"Faded Rose"

THE CONSOLERS OF MIAMI, FLORIDA,
"Waiting For My Child To Come Home"

CANDI STATON,
"That's All You Need"

DOTTIE PEOPLES,
"He's An On-time God"

EVELYN TURRENTINE,
"God Did It"

MIGHTY CLOUDS OF JOY,
"Somewhere Around The Throne"

NATIONAL BAPTIST HYMNAL,
"Yes, Jesus Loves Me"

THE O'NEAL TWINS,
"The Potter"

("Tired"; "I Love To Praise Him" ; Writer(s) not known)

FOREWORD

Several years ago I wrote and directed a Mother's Day play for my church. The play was written as an *operetta* composed of some dialogue, songs and narration. Those who witnessed it enthusiastically applauded it and for many years afterwards as Mother's Day approached, they pleaded with me to do the play again. It was done in a church on the Fort Devens, Massachusetts Army Base for the Patriots Congregation. The Base was huge; actors, singers and musicians were plentiful. Soon after the play, however, the base closed and the talents I had accessed were transferred to other bases. Their performance was superb and I shall never forget them.

Something happened at the production, which leads me to believe that the play was *divinely inspired.* After the play was over that evening I was surrounded by several people who offered congratulations and were saying how much they had enjoyed it, when suddenly a young man pushed through the crowd and excitedly said to me, "Ms Flo, there's a guy outside and he wants to see you!" I said, "OK, tell him I'll be there in a minute." He grabbed my hand and began to literally pull me away. "No! You have to come NOW! He's crying and he's very upset!" I apologized to the people, excused myself and followed the young man outside. The young man took me to the person and I was very moved by what I heard. He was too overcome with tears to talk, his fiancée told me his story. He was a soldier stationed at Ft. Devens. Having witnessed the play, hearing me sing the song "How Long Has It Been Since You Been Home," he was condemned in his spirit for he had not seen his mother in *ten years!* He was determined to confess this to me before heading to Logan Airport in Boston to get a flight to go and see his mother. That moment is unforgettable for it made me realize that "A Rose For Mama" was truly Holy Ghost inspired. I am also convinced that there are many other young men – women, too - who are guilty and need to repent for the wrongs they have done to their mother or father. "Honor thy father and thy mother" is the first commandment with promise. It promises long life to those who will obey it.

I promised the Lord that before I die I would put the play into book form, thereby making it accessible to everyone. *It just might be a blessing to someone* the way it blessed the young man mentioned above. God has never failed in His promises to me and I thank Him that He has blessed me to be true to my promise to Him. *All the glory and all the praise belong to the Lord.*

Be blessed.

CHILDREN, obey your parents in the Lord
[*as His representatives*], for this is just and
right. Honor (esteem and value as precious)
your father and your mother---this is the first
commandment with a promise---[Exod.20:12.]
That all may be well with you and that you may
Live long on the earth. (Eph. 6:1-3; Amp. Bible)

A ROSE FOR MAMA

Lillie and Joe had been sweethearts since their teens and planned to get married as soon as they saved up enough money. Neither of them had much education. In the early 1900's, if you were African American living in the south and fortunate enough to get through high school and college, your neighbors called you "rich and well-to-do." Joe and Lillie were not among the fortunate ones. They were forced to drop out of school after the sixth grade and therefore, forced to work for meager wages. Nevertheless, they saved a few pennies every week. They were not saving for a big wedding; they were saving to buy a little house to live in after they were married. But, as the saying goes, "The best laid plans of mice and men".. or something like that, their plans had to be put on hold when the United States went to war. It was a terrible disappointment to them, they had no living relatives; they had only each other. Joe was among the first to be inducted into the army. They grew up in strict Christian homes and had long ago decided that they would be virgins when they got married; they would live only for each other as long as they lived. Lillie wasn't worried about Joe not coming back to her; she had read in the Bible in Mark 11:24, "Therefore, I say to you, whatever things you ask when you pray, believe that you receive them and you will have them." She said, "The Word of God said it, I believe it, and that settles it." As far as she was concerned she had prayed that her Joe would come back to her alive and well and God was going to answer her prayer. That was her profound confidence in His Word.

After boot camp Joe was sent overseas first to England and then to North Africa. There was a long period of time when the fighting became so fierce he was unable to write to her. Lillie kept on praying that God would "bring my Joe back home safely." She remained loyal to their love for each other and even when Joe's outfit was engaged in fierce fighting and the money stopped coming, it was tough and hard to save, but Lillie kept on working and saving as much as she could. Their little bank account was soon not so little any more; it was growing steadily. Finally she received notice from the army that Joe had been injured and was being sent back to the states to recuperate. Joe had no family. He had named Lillie as the person to be notified in case of his injury or death. As soon as they let her know where he was hospitalized, Lillie boarded a bus and went to be with him. She did not know how serious his injuries were, she was just so thankful that he was alive! As the bus roared down the highway, taking her ever closer to the only man she had ever loved, all she could think about was the many times she had cried and prayed to God that He would take care of Joe and bring him back to her. God was good. He had answered her prayers. Although he was injured, she thought, "God, I thank You that You brought my Joe back home alive!" Several hours of riding the bus and she arrived at the army base. To her delight the army had reserved a room for her in the guesthouse close to the hospital. " God is still blessing me," she thought to herself, "cause I sho' didn't know where I was gon' sleep!"   At the hospital the doctors brought her up to date on Joe's injuries. He had been severely injured, shot several times and lost a lot of blood. They told her that he would never be the man he that he once was. He would need several weeks of intense medical treatment and after that he would need outpatient therapy. "Well, at least he's alive and with God's help he gon' be all right," she told the doctors. She stayed with Joe as long as she could; then she went back home, with hope in her heart and loving him more than she ever did.

Joe's total recovery was slow. It seemed like years before he came home from the hospital; it seemed even longer for him to get strong enough to work. Finally he did get well enough, however, and they got married and moved into their own little cinderblock house. It wasn't much but they were proud of themselves because they had sacrificed, worked hard, and bought their own home with their own money! It wasn't long before Lillie gave birth to their first child, a boy. They named him Michael after the Angel. He was the apple of his father's eye. Joe was always teaching his son something; most of all, he was always telling him, "You must grow up and be strong. Go to school, get an education and be somebody. And if anything happens to me, you have to take over and be the man of the house. You see how I take care of your Mama? That's how you have to take care of her if something happens to me, understand?" Lillie gave birth to a girl two years later. Joe named her Christina and told Lillie, "We gon' call her 'Tina. " "How come we got to call her Tina?" Lillie questioned him. "Cause Negroes always name their girls, Susie or Mary, or Lucy or something like that. Those names come from slavery days. My daughter ain't no slave! "Tina" is a pretty name just like she is," he told his wife." I met a family over in England, they had a little girl named "Tina" and I said if I ever have a girl I was gon' name her Tina." "Honey," Lillie assured him, "She's your daughter, you can name her whatever you want to name her," The third child was a boy two years later. They named him David, after King David in the Bible, of course, because he was going to be a smart man, valiant like the David in the Bible.

The years passed, the children grew "like weeds" as the saying goes. Joe worked unceasingly; Lillie also worked, taking the children to work with her at the suggestion of her employer for whom she worked as a domestic. The kids would help her do her work as much as they could do at their young age, but Lillie was grateful that her boss-lady allowed them to play in her backyard whenever Lillie was busy cooking supper or something like that.
 One day Joe came home from work complaining of a dreadful headache. Lillie gave him aspirin, which gave him no relief at all. Late that night the pain became so severe Lillie took him to the hospital. He was admitted for treatment. The next day he passed away. Lillie thought his illness was probably from his war injuries, which he had never really overcome; but she was told that he had a tumor on his brain, which had apparently been there for sometime and was inoperable.

Lillie's world was shattered but she was a strong woman. More importantly, she was a Christian. She pulled herself up on her most holy faith and vowed to raise her children in the way she and Joe had talked about so many times. The children were 6, 8 and 10 years old. Her job didn't pay much but she counted it a blessing that she had worked for the same family since before she and Joe were married and the family had always been very kind to her. The family had supported her through Joe's hospitalization during the war and they were with her now through the loss of her husband, assuring her that they would continue to support her, that she and her children were not alone.

The sun was setting in the western sky when Lillie got off the city bus. She would need to walk three more blocks to get to the small cinderblock house she called home. Bone tired from working on her domestic job since 6:30AM, her feet were heavy and she was in no hurry. Once she got home her work would begin all over again anyway.

She was one among thousands of young black women in the United States who, in the deep south, had little or no formal education; consequently, the only employment available to them was as a domestic. But Lillie was strong, determined and proud. She was determined to keep her family together; determined that by no means would they live off welfare or beg for anything. When the children would grumble, telling her what other kids had and compare it with what they had or did not have she would firmly chastise them: "Don't you tell me what them other children got, I ain't *their* mama, I'm *yo'* mama and I'm doing the best I can for you. *We may be po' but we ain't pitiful!*" She was the daughter of a Baptist preacher who was a very proud man. She would often attribute her characteristic to him for although her father was a poor man, almost completely illiterate, he would never ask for help to take care of his family. He was out of work more often than he worked, but somehow the family always had enough to eat and a place to stay. It is understandable then, that she would take on the responsibility of head of her family with the same proud attitude.

It was dark by the time she got home. As she took off her shoes and poured the dirt out on the doorsteps, she could hear scurrying around inside the house. It was the kids hurrying to get things in order before she entered the house. She thought to herself, "Children! What can you do wit' em? I know they been in there foolin' around all the afternoon and now they hear me comin' and they trying to do what they shoulda' already done." She had mixed feelings. In one way it was kinda cute. After all, they were just kids. On the other hand she was tired and really didn't feel like fussing at them. She went inside to an empty living room. They had vanished!

"Hey in heah, where is everybody?"

"We're in the kitchen, Mama," Tina, the second oldest yelled back.

Lillie put her bags down and slowly walked to the kitchen surveying the house as she walked along. The house was not tidy but knowing how their mother felt about a dirty kitchen, they were in the kitchen trying to get the dishes washed and the kitchen cleaned up. That was the most important thing. Lillie's pet peeve was to have to cook a meal with dirty dishes everywhere and they knew it! Well, at least they were at home and not out in the streets doing God knows what. Tina was feverishly trying to wash the dishes while David, the youngest boy, sat at the kitchen table doing his homework. Lillie stood there not saying a word but the kids knew what she was thinking. Right away David spoke up apologetically

"Mama, I'm sorry the house isn't cleaned up. I've got a ton of homework to turn in tomorrow and I've been working on it all afternoon; but I did rake up the leaves in the front yard, though."

Lillie gave him a gentle pat on his shoulder, "Alright, honey, you go 'head on and study."

"And what you got to say for yo'self, Miss Queen Bee?" she asked Tina.

Well, she just should not have asked that question. Tina went on a tirade that sounded like a confession of guilt combined with an 'I'm not supposed to be here, this is beneath me,' attitude.

"When I got home from school I was tired from carrying all those big ol' books. Then I spent I don't know long looking for my earrings that I couldn't find this morning before I left for school. I can never find anything of mine in this house; somebody is always moving my stuff. I don't have but two or three pairs of earrings and I always have to search for them every time I want to put them on. I have no privacy; my brothers go into my room and take my things without asking me; they go through my drawers – I don't know what they be looking for – and leave my clothes all tumbled up. It's ridiculous!"

Looking up from his book in horror, David said, "Girl, you must be outta your mind! I never go in your room, let alone go in your drawers. What would you have in your drawers that I would want? I'm no girl!"

"You or Michael one goes in my room and messes up my things! " Tina yelled back.

"Well, you better yell at Michael 'cause it wasn't me!"

Lillie realized she'd better intervene before things got any hotter. "Just take it easy, young lady, I'll talk to Michael about it. Did he get home from school yet?"

"I don't know, I haven't seen him," David said.

"School? What school? Michael don't go to nobody's school," Tina answered.

Lillie looked at her daughter in amazement. "What you talking 'bout, Michael don't go to school?"

"I mean he goes when he wants to and when he don't want to he don't,"

"Well how come somebody ain't told me?"

"It's not my business; he's older than I am, I can't tell him what to do. Besides, I've got to keep my mind focused on *my* own future, on that doctor or lawyer I'm gonna marry so I won't have to go through this kind of junk like you're going through. I am not gonna have no children to worry my life and I sure am not going to have to wash no stupid dishes!!" She angrily slammed the wet dishrag down on the counter. Lillie looked at her daughter and shaking her head she silently mused, "God help the man that marries that girl"

"Child, hush your mouth and get thru with them dishes so I can make ya'll sumpn' to eat. Lawd! I am *so* tired."

She sat down wearily at the kitchen table where David was doing his homework. Quizzically she eyed the books for a moment then asked him, "Baby, what is all them books, what you have to study 'em for?"

"Well, this one is a biology manual; it's the study of anatomy, the human body. This one is a chemistry book, the study of science."

"Uh huh. What you say that other one was, 'ah-nat-uh' what?"

"You mean the biology book?"

"Yeah, that one right there," pointing to the book.

"It's called biology, the study of the human body," He sensed she was not understanding what he was saying. He looked into her questioning eyes and told her. "Mama, this is too deep for you and its way over your head; don't try to understand it."

His mother gave him a smile that told him she was very proud of him. "You sho' got that right, baby; mama sho'nuff don't understand it. It's way over mama's head!"

Embarrassed for his mother, the boy replied, "If you want to be a doctor you have to study it, that's all I'm saying."

"That's good, honey, you go right ahead and study it. Someday I know my baby gon' be a real good doctor, make lots of money. Mama gon' be so proud o' you, switching round in the hospital with that long white coat on and that thing hangin' round yo' neck. You gon' be one good lookin' doctor! And I'll be standin' over there somewhere lookin' at you and sayin' to myself, 'that's my baby!' Lawd, I sho' do wish your daddy coulda' lived to see you be a doctor. He sho' woulda been proud o' you."

David could tell that his mother was about to start crying like she always did when she talked about their father, so he smiled broadly and said, "Well, then I guess I'll just have to be twice as good, all for you, Mama."

She choked back the tears. "Aw, you go 'head and study your lesson, honey, Mama got to git you all somethin' to eat." She turned her back to him to hide the tears that were filling her eyes. She couldn't help herself. Her husband had been dead for several years but he had been her first and only love; she loved him just as much today as when they first got married. He had been such a good husband and a wonderful father, the only man she had ever been intimate with. But she had no time to reminisce she had to make dinner for the kids and try and get some rest and start all over again tomorrow.

Lillie, Tina and David sat down to eat. Lillie listened as the children recounted their day at school and could not help being proud of them. Tina was a pretty girl intent upon becoming an actress or, in the alternative, to marry a successful lawyer or doctor. David was going to be a doctor, no question about it. And Michael ...well, Michael was going to be *Michael*. He was a smart boy, had a good mathematical brain and good with his hands, at fixing things just like his daddy. He was supposed to graduate from high school this year but the way he was skipping classes he probably wouldn't make it. Lately, he wouldn't help around the house leaving the hardest chores for poor little David and his sister to do. It bothered his mother a lot but there was not much she could do about it. He was almost 18 years old. Before his father died he would talk to Michael about being "the man of the house" after his father died. Did Michael do like his father told him to do? No, not even close. All Lillie could do was pray that he would someday change his ways.

Suddenly the kitchen door opened and Michael sauntered in.

"Michael, where in the world have you been?"

He arrogantly answered, "Around."

"Around? Around where, and wit who?"

"With my boys, that's who!"

"Did you go to school today?" She eyed him suspiciously.

"Aw, Mama, don't start in on me about no school. School ain't nothing but a waste of time and a rip-off for Negroes. They break their behinds going to school and study all their life, then they get the almighty degree and none of them white folks will hire 'em. They still have to be bellhops, wait tables or clean some white folks' yards out in that hot sun or something. So what's the use?"

"Times is changin', child. When you get grown and have to make a living for yo'self it won't be like it is today; but you haf' ta' go to school and get a' education, son!"

Michael looked at his mother, his eyes blazing, "Mama, look; I be in the streets, I see how Negroes are being treated. I mean, people who got a high school education or even a college degree can't get a good job; they're out there working in them white folks' houses, cleaning their yards or fixing their homes; some even dig ditches. Well, I ain't gon' spend my time studying for somethin I ain't never gon' be able to get nothin' out of. I can make more money in the streets than I could with a college degree!"

Lillie sprang to her feet. "Boy, what in the world is you talkin' about?"

Michael reached into his pocket and pulled out a roll of ten and $20 bills, proudly displaying them. "This is what *I'm* talking about!"

Lillie almost fainted! Her hands flew up to her throat like somebody was choking her as she stared at the money in horrified disbelief! "O, my God! Boy, where in the world did you get all that money?"

As if he wanted to make the most of this *"out of the closet"* moment, he took his wallet from his back pocket and emptied several more $20 and $50 bills on the table.

"I had more than this but I had to give my homeboys somethin' for their work," he explained.

Lillie could tell that he was proud of whatever it was he had done to get all that money and it frightened her.

"You mind tellin' me what kind of *work* your *homeboys* did for you for all that money?"

The boy sighed, looked at his mother for a moment, then shrugging his shoulders and walking away from her, he told her, "Mama, you really don't want me to tell you that."

"Um-huh, thas' just what I thought. If you did something good to get it you wouldn't mind me knowin' what it was. Boy, you is on yo' way to jail, do you know that?"

"No I ain't going to no jail, either! I know how to take care of myself, I ain't no fool!"

Such a feeling of utter helplessness came over Lillie. This was her firstborn, her firstborn son for whom her husband, in his lifetime, had so many dreams. He looked so much like his father. But the words coming out of his mouth this day were unbelievable! She silently prayed that God would give her the words to say to her son to turn him around. "Son, whatever you doin' I don't have no idea what it is, but it is wrong. Ain't' nothing you could do in one day to make that much money. I know that. How come you cain't do the work like your daddy did before he died?"

"Like my daddy did? Mama, you got to be crazy! That's how come he's dead; he worked himself to death for them white people, for nothing. I sure don't plan to do that."

"Michael, if you want money that bad you can do more 'round the house to help me out and I'll give you some money, even if I have to get another job," she said, tears streaming down her cheeks.

"If you worked two jobs and gave me all the money you made it still wouldn't be as much as this. And working 'round this house – that ain't my bag. I don't plan on killing myself for you and nobody else." He was so defiant, so unlike the son she had known for almost 18 years. As she looked at him memories of her pregnancy, his very early childhood and the plans she and his father had in mind for their firstborn, flashed before her.

For the nine months I carried you, growing inside me,
No charge;
For the nights I sat up with you, doctored you, prayed for you,
No charge.
For the time and the tears and the cost through the years,
There's no charge, son.
When you add it all up the full cost of my love is
No charge
For the nights filled with dread, and the worries ahead,
No charge.
For advice and the knowledge and the cost of your college,
No charge.
For the toys, food and clothes and for wiping your nose
There's no charge, son
When you add it all up, the full cost of my love is
No charge.

"Son, I wish with all my heart and every drop of blood thas' running thru' my veins that you could understand what you're doing with your life. You are too young to throw your life away on that foolishness you talking about. You got a good head on yo' shoulders. You need to go to college and make sump'n out of yourself. There's plenty of good colleges 'round heah', they would be glad to have a boy like you. Michael, honey, I'm begging you; don't throw your life away. Please don't throw your life away!"

"You can give all that knowledge and college 'BS' to David, wit' his little fagot self. I don't need it. I can make it by myself. I don't need your help!"

Michael stormed out of the house; slamming the door behind him so hard it shook the house! Lillie made no effort to stop him. She sat down, her head in her hands, and cried like a baby. Tina and David stood there looking at each other not knowing what to say or do to comfort her. They put their arms around her. David, being a boy, simply said, "Mama, don't cry." Tina, being a female with instilled maternal instincts that could not be silenced, blurted out, "I really don't know what you're crying and making yourself sick for over an idiot like Michael. He ain't nothing but a fool. Let him go!! When he gets out there and them thugs kick his black behind he'll come back. But I don't care if he never comes back. Good riddance, I say!"

"That's alright; he's young and don't understand what he's doing. I'll just keep on praying for him, turn it over to the Lord and He'll fix it. I know I did everything I know to do for him, I don't know what else to do."

> *When everything you ever worked for,*
>
> *Is gone, in a second;*
>
> *When life throws you a curve you can't bend.*
>
> *When the world has turned against you*
>
> *And all your so-called friends forsake you*
>
> *When there's nothing left but God*
>
> *That's all you need.*

Several minutes later, and after a lot more tears, she calmed down and got control of herself. She hugged the two children, thanked them for their comfort and what they considered encouragement, then she went into her bedroom, got on her knees and prayed. She prayed that God would forgive Michael's sins, save him and keep His hedge of protection always around the boy. Her prayer for all of her children had always been for God's hedge of protection around them so that they would always be safe from harm and danger. She understood that some day they would be grown and would go their own way, but she never dreamed that they would leave her the way Michael had done. Nevertheless, he was her son, her child, and she still loved him. "You never stop loving your child no matter what he does," was her old-fashioned country-style philosophy.

The years passed swiftly; too fast it seemed to Lillie. Michael left home and went his own way. She didn't know where he was; he never called or wrote to her. Although he was always in her heart and in her mind, she understood that she had two other children to take care of and to worry about. "No news is good news," she decided. She never stopped praying for him and asking the Lord to send her boy back home so she could see him again before she died; that was all she could do. Outwardly she wore a smile but inwardly her heart was breaking into a million pieces worrying about Michael and at the same time working hard and raising two teenagers. All these things were taking their toll on her physically and mentally. Her steps were slowing and her thick jet-black hair was now being invaded by that white stuff called "gray." The pain of arthritis was becoming more frequent and more severe. Still she never wavered in her determination to take care of her home and her children, never missing a day's work. Tina helped out by baby-sitting and earning money to buy the little things that teenage girls feel they just must have and can't live without. Whenever David was not in the library or the science lab at school, he took care of the yards and the rose beds and the other things that needed to be done for the house. They didn't have a lot of amenities like some other people have but there was an awful lot of love in the house and they were happy. Michael's deserting them seemed to bring them closer together.

Two years after Michael left home Tina graduated from high school and went off to Hampton Institute with the help of the people Lillie had worked for so many years. She had been active in school plays, dancing, and fine arts throughout high school. In college she majored in fine arts taking part in stage plays on campus. When she graduated, it was the proudest day of her mother's life. Two years after Tina's graduation from high school, David graduated from high school with honors. Valedictorian of his class and at the top of the Honor Roll, he was offered a full scholarship to Morehouse College – now both children were college students. When Tina walked across that platform and received her BA Degree, Lillie experienced a joy that she never dreamed possible! She was so proud of her only daughter. No parent could have been happier. Then, for her youngest to graduate with all those honors and a full scholarship to Morehouse College! "I am not just blessed, I am *better* than blessed!" she told herself. She was proud, yet humble, for she knew where the blessings had come from. They came from the Lord.

After graduation Tina could not find work in her chosen field. After all, she lived in the south where the arts were meant *'for whites only.'* So she finally decided to go to Los Angeles where she had friends that she had met in college and a better chance of getting a role in a movie or stage play. Tina came home for David's graduation but there was still no word from Michael. Nobody had heard from him since the night he walked out of her house. Lillie still loved him and still prayed daily that the Lord would take care of him and send him back home to her so she could see him again before she died. Tina, on the other hand had stayed in constant touch with her mother after she moved to California. Although she had not been successful in her bid for movies, she still had the faith. In the meantime, she had landed a well-paying position with a production company and was doing very well for herself, financially. She often sent money home to her mother to help with expenses at home. Tina was so proud of her "little brother," as she called David. One day while she was home, Lillie overheard the two of them discussing how they were going to take care of her. "Mama is getting old, and that arthritis in her knees and in her back is getting worse. I can see the pain in her face but she just won't stop working just like she has done all our lives. I wish I could persuade her to come out to LA with me. I'm making enough money to take care of both of us now; but I know she won't leave here no matter what, especially now with you still having to intern for a million years before you can go into practice."

"Yeah, I know. It's a shame that nobody has found a cure for arthritis and diabetes and those ailments that old people in particular suffer from. They're working on it, maybe one day soon someone will discover a cure. Maybe it will be me, who knows? In the meantime, I will certainly keep on top of any pain relievers that will at least make the pain a little more bearable. Mama has given her whole life to her children. We are truly blessed to have a mother like her. It's gonna be a long time, doctors don't start making money as soon as they get out of college; they still have to go through internship and setting up a practice. All of that takes time and a lot of money! But as soon as I can I am going to take Mama out of all this, buy her a house – a real nice house – with all the modern equipment that will make her life comfortable and she won't have to work anymore."

Tina told him (teasing him), "I'll tell you what, if I can get her to come and live with me until you get your practice set up, you can build *both* of us a house since you'll be making so much money. OK?"

"Sure, sure, Sis! you can count on it." Both of them burst out laughing.

"Seriously, though, buying Mama a nice house someday is at the top of my agenda. God being my helper, I will do it."

Tina gave him a real big hug. She was so proud of him.

"One thing *you* have to do, Tina." She rolled her eyes, put her hands on her hips and invited him, "Lay it on me, baby."

"You got to quit calling me *Little Brother*."

"What!! Why you little son-of-a-gun, are you trying to get snobbish on me already? You'll *always* be my little brother, you got that? I don't care how many medical degrees you get"

"I am your *youngest* brother ..."

"My *little* brother."

"Aw Tina, come on, you know what I mean. How do you think I'd feel if you came around my colleagues and they heard you calling me that? They'd call me a wimp or something. So please, just call me by my name, OK?"

Tina thought, "He's so cute." She stepped back, gushing with pride and assured him, "You got it baby, I would never embarrass you before *anybody*! I'm too proud of you. I just can't believe it, my little brother has grown up, trying to be a *man*, and a little smart ass, too!"

David shook his head as if to say "There is no help for this girl" and left her laughing her head off. The kids were so happy and showed such love for each other. Hearing them teasing each other and talking seriously about their love for her made her feel very humble and thankful to God for guiding them, raising them up to be a fine respectable young man and young woman. Lillie could not believe what was happening. It was too good to be true. She had three children and two of them were college graduates. Imagine that! Their mother and father had barely finished elementary school! God had truly blessed them. At that moment her son Michael's face flashed before her as always and her mood instantly changed to sadness. Tina and David came into the room and seeing the sad look on her face, asked, "Mama, what 's the matter?"

> *I was talking to a lady, a few days ago;*
> *And these are the words I said: "If you see my*
> *Son somewhere as you travel here and there,*
> *tell him I'm waiting for my child to come home.*
> *I'm waiting, waiting, for my child to come;*
> *I'm waiting, waiting, for my child to come.*
> *If he can't come home, tell him to please*
> *send me a letter.*
> *I'm waiting for my child to come home.*
> *My child may be somewhere on his sick bed,*
> *and there's no one to rub his aching head.*
> *My child could be somewhere in some*
> *lonely jail, and there's no one to go his bail.*
> *If I only knew what town my child was in,*
> *I'd go there on that early morning train.*
> *And no matter what the crime, I'd tell the judge,*
> *"This child is mine."*
> *I'm waiting for my child to come home.*
> .

"Mama, do you mean you been trying to get people to help you find Michael?" Tina asked.

"Sho' I have. I ain't shame of it neither. No matter what he's done he is still my child. I would do the same thing for ya'll, too."

They looked at each other. They had seen their mother in this kind of mood many times through the years. Lillie was *that* kind of mother. Someone once said that no matter how bad a child is, a real mother will always see some good in him. Everybody else might give up on him but a real mother will remain steadfast in her love for her child. So it was with Lillie. In her heart she held a faith picture of the day when she would see her son Michael again. It had been six years since he left home and still no word from him since he left. He seemed to have vanished into thin air. Nevertheless, she kept on praying, stubbornly holding fast to God's promise:

> "For assuredly, I say to you, whoever says to this mountain, 'Be removed and be cast into the sea,' and does not doubt in his heart, but believes that those things he says will be done, he will have whatsoever he says. Therefore, I say to you, whatever things you ask when you pray, believe that you receive them, and you will have them." (Mark 11:23,24; NKJV)

She had been praying all those years that God would take care of her son, save him, and send him back home to her. And no matter what anybody said, or how long it would take, she believed that God would do it for her.

When Tina moved away and David was finishing college Lillie was left alone in the house that held so many memories; the house where she and her husband spent all the years of their marriage; where her children were born and grew up, where her husband had died. Now they were all gone. It got mighty lonely sometime. She still had her friends at church. They had been like family to her, even more now that the kids were gone. Although the arthritis got worse every day making it more painful to bend or stoop, she took great pleasure in her rose beds, still planted them and took care of them. She truly had the 'green thumb' when it came to her roses. Perhaps it was because she loved them so much, like her children. There was some pain from time to time when she was raising them but the rewards were much greater than the pain. Just like the thorns on the rose bushes pricked her hands and caused them to bleed and become sore, the children's actions sometime caused pain in her heart. But just like the roses, her children were a labor of love and O' so beautiful to her! Her roses became somewhat of a symbol of Lillie. On Sunday there was always a vase of her home grown roses in the pulpit beside the podium. The pastor would remark, "Sister McClendon, these roses are so beautiful, just like you."

Tina called her mother often and made weekend trips home as often as possible. She still sent money home always begging her mother to stop working, but Lillie stubbornly refused. Tina met a man in the music industry who owned a small but fast growing record company and the relationship had become quite serious. His headquarters were in New York City so they spent a lot of time commuting back and forth between Los Angeles and New York City. This continued for a long time. All the while Tina was very worried about her mother getting up in age and living alone. Even with the arthritis that bothered her, Lillie was still her own woman, determined and headstrong. After several months of flying back and forth Tina and her boyfriend, Alvin, got married and decided to live in New York City. Her husband gave her an executive position in his record company and they became quite successful. They pleaded with Lillie to come and live with them but as usual she declined their offer. Tina still frequently sent money to her mother and would fuss at her for continuing to work. But Lillie would always say in rebuttal, "I been wit' the Thompsons so long til it ain't no job. It's like goin' home when I go there. They just like my family. In fact, they told me if I want to move they will fix me up a 'partment up over their garage and I can stay there. Tina could in no way understand the wisdom in that. But that was her mother - whatever made her happy , as hardheaded as she was.

David finished medical school and began his internship in a large hospital in a town about a hundred miles away. He had dated a girl while he was in college, she had gotten pregnant and they secretly got married. Gloria, David's wife, had majored in education and had her degree. Naturally, Lillie was hurt and disappointed that David had kept it a secret from her but there was nothing she could do about it and so she accepted it gracefully like she always accepted things over which she had no control. That was one of her many assets. The plan was that Gloria would get a teaching job and support the family while David did his internship. David brought his wife home to live with his mother until the baby's arrival. The arrangement didn't sit well with Tina at all.

"My mother is too old to be taking care of anybody's baby. What the hell is David thinking about?"

Lillie had several good reasons why the arrangement made perfect sense. Gloria's family lived hundreds of miles away and she and David are married with a baby, her first grandchild, on the way and they want to be close to each other like any other young married couple. Besides, it wouldn't be any expenses living with David's mom and they could save toward a home of their own..

"I cannot understand for the life of me why mama won't sell that damn old house and come and live here with us," Tina told her husband.

"Well, I told her if she would come and live with us I'll build an apartment for her above the garage or I can make it an attachment to the house. She could have her privacy and we would be close by to see to her needs. I guess she's just happier in her own home no matter how old it is. That's how old people are. Honey, if your mother is happy where she is, leave her alone, let her be happy, OK?" Tina reluctantly dropped the subject for the time being.

Gloria moved in with her mother-in-law and a new life began for Lillie. This was her first daughter-in-law and she was expecting Lillie's first grandchild. It really was a new life. Gloria and her unborn child were both diagnosed as healthy. Her pregnancy was uncomplicated. She found a teaching position at one of the schools in town. David came home as often as he could. The arrangement worked well, Gloria and Lillie got along well although every now and then Lillie got the feeling that her daughter-in-law was "looking down her nose" at her --- like she was better than her mother-in-law.

After she had lived there for a few months Gloria began to find fault with the way Lillie kept her house, the way she cooked and the way she talked. She would often make comments like, "My mother doesn't do it like that", or, "I don't want you to use those words around my child, they're not good English." Lillie just shrugged off the comments and kept on doing what she had always done. For the most part she felt that the young woman was just young and inexperienced, never had any responsibilities and was college educated, so naturally they would be quite different. Lillie figured she could tolerate Gloria as long as she loved her son and treated him right. That's all that mattered.

Soon, a healthy little baby boy, David, Jr., was born and that brought another change. At first Gloria was very possessive, doing everything for the baby. Lillie did the dirty work. She made the bottles, washed the baby's clothes and changed the soiled diapers, but the loving and hugging and cuddling were only for the child's parents. Lillie was more like the housemaid than the grandmother. It wasn't easy. She often felt unappreciated, like nobody cared about her or her feelings. Tina had her husband and her career and David had his family and his career; she was still praying that she would soon hear from Michael but she still did not have the slightest idea where he was or if he was still alive. Deep in her heart of hearts, though, faith was keeping hope alive and she simply refused to believe that God would not someday answer her prayer and send her son home to her. She had only memories. But when Gloria went back to work Lillie quit her job and stayed home to take care of the baby. That worked out fine, for then she had lots of time to spend hugging and cuddling him. Neighbors and church members would stop by from time to time and talk with her concerning her life and about how she was getting along. She would merely tell them, "The Lord's been good to me and I thank Him for it. Sometime when I look around me it looks like everybody loves somebody except me. But, like Apostle Paul wrote in Philippians the 4th Chapter and the 11th verse: "...*I have learned in whatever state I'm in, to be content."* I can do that because I know this one thing:

> *Jesus loves me, this I know; for the Bible tells me so.*
> *Little ones to Him belong, they are weak but He is*
> *Strong. (that's why I can say)*
> *Yes, Jesus loves me, Oh...*
> *Yes, Jesus loves me,*
> *Yes, Jesus loves me, I know, I know, I know because*
> *The Bible tells me so.*

When David finished his internship he opened a private practice. He and Gloria worked hard and soon were able to buy their own home. It was a beautiful house with lots of rooms set on a huge plot of land in the countryside. With their success and social standing and because of Lillie's age and declining health, they persuaded her to sell her house and move in with them as a live-in Nanny. It seemed like a good idea at the time since, in her mind, she would be close to her grandchildren and at the same time be in the home with family. Things went well. David had more rooms added to the ground floor of the house so that his mother could have her privacy without having to climb the stairs to get to her quarters. She had her own little apartment consisting of a bedroom, a sitting room that served as a livingroom, a kitchenette and bathroom. It was on the rear of the house where she could look out across the meadows and see people riding their horses. There was so much space between their house and a neighbor's house until the only way you would know that someone else lived in the vicinity was to see the rooftop in the distance. At these times a warm feeling of pride and gratitude to God would come over her. She thought of how diligently David had studied when he was growing up, determined to be a doctor. "Well, all that determination sure did pay off," she would say. She could not help but feel very proud of him; he was gaining so much recognition in the field of medicine, still worked very hard. In addition to his private practice he also did research and was away from home a lot working in the lab at the hospital. David had always been very sensitive to the needs of others. It bothered him to see someone in pain. He seemed to think that for every pain there had to be a cure somewhere and that it was *his* responsibility to find it. Because he worked so tirelessly, he was highly respected by his peers and had been awarded numerous awards for his work. There had even been talk of a nomination for the prestigious Nobel Peace Prize. It did not happen, but she was still proud of him. She would smile and say, "That's my baby. I always knew he would be somebody!"

David and Gloria had three more children, two girls and another boy. It really seemed like those kids were Lillie's own children instead of her grandchildren. David was gone most of the time taking care of his private practice and doing his lab work. Gloria, even though she had three more babies, had managed to get her master's degree and a doctorate in education. So now she wasn't teaching anymore. She had been appointed Assistant Superintendent of Schools earning a huge annual salary. Yes, they had made it, alright. In fact, they had left the household supervision to Lillie. They hired a housekeeper and a cook so all Lillie had to do was tell them what to do and watch the children. They were growing up so fast. Too fast! Lillie's health and age were working against her. The three older children were well up in grade school now and involved in various school activities; the younger one was as energetic as a dozen kids, a real handful for her. It had begun to take its toll on her physically although she wouldn't admit it. Many times she would fall asleep while watching the children play. Her steps were getting slower, arthritis had made its way in to every joint in her body. She was in pain most of the time but never told her doctor/son who lived in the same house with her. Of course, she hardly ever saw him. Lillie soon found out that the children were reporting to their parents about her. David and Gloria came to see her and David examined her as best he could at home. The next day he made an appointment with a colleague of his instructing him to do a thorough physical examination.

The doctor performed an extensive examination as David had requested including tests that were long overdue. His report was not real good but it was not all that bad for a woman her age. Her ailments, for the most part, were conducive with a woman her age. Along with the arthritis, she was diabetic, had high-blood pressure and a slight hearing impairment. She was overweight, had been for many years, and the doctor emphasized that she must loose the excess weight. Although these things were common in the elderly, to Lillie it was devastating! She had been having some pain for a long time; but she had felt more tired than anything else. Her joints ached especially in cloudy weather – but other than that she felt she was in good health for her age.

"You must take better care of yourself. No heavy lifting or climbing. Your joints aren't as strong as they once were and you must take care not to fall because if you break your bones they will not heal as fast or as well as they used to," the doctor explained.

"I don't climb no stairs, I don't do no heavy lifting. My grandchillun's too big for me to lift 'em now. The only thing I do is take care o' my roses. They ain't heavy, I love them!"

It was not difficult for him to understand that she loved taking care of her roses; she spoke of them with such compassion.

"Only thing is, "I cain't git up and down like I used to. It's hard gittin' down and it's harder gittin' up. My back hurts awful!"

The young man searched for a way to make her understand that her back hurts because arthritis had "set up housekeeping" in her back, her spine was now old and brittle. God forbid that he should say something to insult or make this beautiful old lady feel uncomfortable. He remembered that rose bushes have thorns so he admonished her.

"Mrs. McClendon, I understand how much you must love your roses, but I must impress upon you that you are diabetic and no matter how beautiful the roses are they have thorns and when you are out there taking care of them you run the risk of pricking your fingers or getting scratched by the thorns. Those small breaks or bruises to your skin can be very harmful to a diabetic."

She gazed up at him thoughtfully. "When you love sumpn' you might git hurt sometime but you don't quit lovin' 'em or quit takin' care of 'em; you keeps on lovin' 'em, you keeps on doin' all you can for 'em; your love hides the pain and you don't even feel the hurt, because you love 'em so much. My roses don't have nobody to love 'em or take care of 'em but me. I cain't let 'em down."

The doctor was speechless. He could not think of a worthwhile response; all he could say was, "Well, when you're taking care of your roses, just be sure to wear cotton gloves and long sleeves to protect your flesh from the thorns, OK?"

A revealing smile lit up her face. He noticed and asked, "Do you like to wear gloves?"

"No, it ain't the gloves. When you talked about protecting my flesh from the thorns, I was just thinking 'bout what Apostle Paul said about the thorn in the Bible. You ever read it? About his thorn in the flesh?"

He thought for a moment and replied, "No maam, I don't believe I have.

That did it!

"You see, Apostle Paul was goin' round from place to place preachin' and tellin' folks about Jesus. They didn't believe him; they beat him, stoned him, tried to kill him but he kept on preaching, tellin' about Jesus. Know why? See, Paul loved the Lawd. God had anointed Paul to preach the Gospel to the Gentile peoples and showed him visions and things that other people couldn't see. When he seen all them visions and things from the Lawd it made him feel big and he wanted to brag about 'em. But he didn't want to be, like he said 'puffed up' or make himself out to be more than other people. He just wanted everybody to see the Lawd like he saw Him. But the more he talked about the Lawd the more people hated him.

He called it a 'thorn in the flesh.' He asked the Lawd three times to remove the thorn but the Lawd told him 'My grace is sufficient . for you.' You mean to tell me you ain't never heard about that in the Bible?" She opened her purse and took out a small Bible that she always carried with her. Handing the bible to the doctor she urged him,

"Turn to Second Corinthians, Chapter 12 and read from verse one down to verse ten."

The young man looked at his watch - he was spending an awful lot of time with his friend's mother, he had other patients to see - but he took the book, opened it to the Scripture she told him to read. He read it, shrugged his shoulders and offered it back to her without comment. He simply told her,

"When you're taking care of your roses, just be sure to wear cotton gloves to protect your hands and arms. I'm going to talk to David about your health and give him the prescriptions for the medicine I want you to take."

She eyed him suspiciously. "You don't understand what you just read, do you? Did you see what the Lawd told Paul 'bout that thorn? Paul said he asked the Lawd three times to move the thorn but God told him, 'My grace is sufficient for you.' God's favor was enough for Paul. If its good 'nuff for Paul, it sho' is good 'nuff for me! I'll do like you said, I'll wear some gloves, but I just want you to know that I ain't scared o' nothing happenin' to me when I'm taking care of my roses. God will take care o' *me and my roses*."

The young doctor smiled respectfully, "Yes, maam. I believe you."

Lillie left the doctor's office and took a seat in one of the chairs on the sidewalk in front of the building to wait for David's driver. Since she hardly ever went anywhere these days except to church, downtown really looked strange to her. It was a warm sunny day and most everybody – at least the young people – all wore shorts or hardly any clothes at all. Looking around, she noticed weird things like two men walking together affectionately holding hands and women doing the same thing. She was amazed at how the world had changed. In her day that kind of stuff would never be seen in public! She shook her head in dismay and softly whispered, "Lawd, in the name o' Jesus, please help 'em cause they don' know what they doing."

David came home late as usual that night. He entered the bedroom quietly trying not to waken Gloria but almost immediately she turned on the bedside lamp and rubbing her eyes to get the sleep out, she greeted her husband, inquired about how his day had been then quickly went right to the question of his mother's doctor's appointment. David told her what his friend said then took a deep breath and waited for the barrage of exclamations that he knew would be coming from his wife. True to form, she did just that.

"How could you let your mother get that sick living in the same house with you!?"

"How can you ask me a question like that? With the long hours I work at the hospital and at the Lab, I don't see her very often. In fact, you see her more than I do!"

"Yes, but you're the doctor, I'm not. I see her when I get home early sometime but she's always asleep or dozing. She even goes to sleep while I'm trying to talk to her. Anyway, --- just tell me what Fred said."

With a weary sigh David proceeded to tell his wife what his friend had said about Lillie's health. When he finished giving her all the details, Gloria exclaimed,

"My God, David, it sounds like your mother needs to have constant care. She needs to be in a nursing home!"

"For heaven's sake, Gloria, don't be so dramatic, Mama's not *that* bad off; she's just going through the things that elderly people go through, especially when they didn't take care of themselves when they were young. Mama worked hard taking care of her children when she was a young woman and didn't have the time or the means to take care of herself. Now that she's old, all the years of neglect to her body are showing up."

David was trying to explain the situation to his wife from a physician's prospective but he was really speaking as a son who had witnessed his mother's struggles through the years. Many days she went to work when she was in pain, as sick as a dog, but she never complained; even when she would have the money to go to a doctor, if one of her children needed something she put her own needs on hold. And she did it with a smile. Her children were always first in her life. Gloria watched her husband intently, realizing that he was reliving his childhood.

"I understand how you feel about your mother, honey, but we have to be realistic. Obviously, your mother is not going to get any better. I've heard you say many times that there is no cure for arthritis and diabetes; the only thing you can do is give people some medicine to make them feel better for a little while but the disease is still there. Now, David, you know that we are raising children and we have our careers to think about. Your mother needs to be somewhere where she can have care around the clock and be with people her own age. Being here with us, she never goes out any more, not even to church, not because she doesn't want to, she just doesn't feel like going anywhere. She doesn't even look after the kids like she used to. And, I know you don't want to hear this but, I am tired of having to correct their English. Your mother uses bad English and the kids imitate it. We are professionals, we can't afford to have our children using such language. If you put her in a nursing home you will be 'killing two birds with one stone' so to speak. She would be getting the care she needs and we could get someone to come in and help us raise our children. Believe me. some girl in college over there who needs help paying her tuition would love to have a job like that. You see what I'm saying?"

Like a man who was both physically and mentally exhausted, David covered his face with his hands, bowed his head and replied, "I know, I know; you want me to put my mother in a nursing home." He dropped his hands from his face and clasping them between his knees he stared at her and defiantly asked, "Do you understand how that looks? That makes it look like I'm throwing my own mother away! I'm sorry, I can't do that. I can't do that to my mother. I promised to take care of her when I became a doctor and I am going to keep that promise!."

Gloria sprang out of bed and just as defiantly, shot back, "I don't care *what* you promised *before* you became a doctor, you are a doctor with a family now and your family comes first before your mama or anybody else! Now, I tried to be nice about this but I have to think about what is best for our children. Your mother has had her life - such as it was, it was hers; now we have to make a life for our children, *they* are our responsibility, *not* your mother! With your contacts at the hospital I know you can find a very nice nursing home for her --- and I strongly suggest that you do it, quick, fast, and in a hurry! Do we understand one another?!" She stormed out of the room, slamming the door behind her, leaving David alone and heartbroken. He could not believe this was happening. He had always glorified his family, believing he had the perfect family. A lovely, brainy and talented wife, four beautiful smart children, a lovely home with all the amenities anyone could ask or wish for. All this was made possible because of an annual six-figure income supplemented by his wife's huge annual salary. And to all this, he always had with him his wonderful caring mother whose treasure of God-given wisdom was always accessible to him. Often he had prayed that the mother of his children would follow his own mother's example and be the loving, understanding, encouraging, compassionate and forgiving mother that Lillie was. Seems like the Good Lord didn't make 'em like that anymore. But he had to keep his mind on the present problem. His heart was not in this task that his wife had demanded. There must be a better way, something else that he could do other than put his mother out of his house. Wearily he sat down on the bed and prayed, "Lord, please show me what to do." He sat there for what seemed like hours before deciding that he must try to get some rest. He would face the problem tomorrow.

Driving into town the next day David's dilemma was uppermost in his mind. He could not get his mother's face out of his mind, how she would look when he told her what he would have to tell her. Suddenly, it was not his mother's face he saw, it was his sister's face!

"Tina! That's it. Why didn't I think of that? Tina's always tried to get Mama to come and stay with her. That's it, she can go there instead of to some nursing home!" This was the solution to his problem! Instead of going first to the hospital for rounds like he usually did, he sped towards his office.

David felt much better. He knew it would be no problem for Tina since she had begged Lillie time and time again to come and live with her.

As soon as he got into his office he told his secretary, "See if you can get my sister on the phone right away." Looking at his watch to check the time, "Try her office first. If she's not there, tell her office to track her down and tell her to call me immediately. It's very important."

A few minutes later the secretary reported, " Your sister's office said she's out of the country, in London, on a business trip. She's not expected back until next week. I told them it's urgent that she contacts you as soon as possible. They said they would track her and relay the message."

"Thank you. If she calls and I'm not here, forward the call to me. It's urgent that I talk to her, understand?"

"Of course. I'll be happy to do that, sir."

It was about a half hour later as David was preparing to go to the hospital to make rounds when his secretary rushed into his office.

"Dr. Mac, your sister's on your private line!"

He picked up the phone excitedly, "Tina, am I glad they got ahold of you. How are you?"

"I was fine until my assistant called me saying I should call you right away. What's wrong? Is something wrong with Mama?"

"Nothing's wrong with Mama but I do need to talk to you about something that I have to do about her."

"Something you have to do about her? What the hell does that mean?"

"Well, long story short, I need you to let Mama live with you."

"O?" (silence) "Come on Lil' Brother, tell me what's happening. Is Gloria kicking your butt out and Mama's got to get out, too?"

"Come on, Tina, I'm not in the mood. This is very serious. I've got to find a home for Mama. Gloria suggested a nursing home but I am not happy with that and I don't believe Mama will be happy with it."

" Wait a minute; am I hearing you right, that Gloria suggested putting Mama in a nursing home?"

"Yeah. But only if she can't, or won't, live with you. I believe she'll agree to live with you. I know you always wanted her to live with you."

"Yes, you're right; I have been trying to get her to live with me for years, but she wouldn't. What makes you think she'll do it now? What the hell's going on over there? What have you people done to my Mama? C'mon, talk to me---- and it better be damn good!"

"Tina, just calm down. Nobody's done anything to *our* Mama. I sent her to my friend, Fred --- I think you met him once when you were visiting home; he did an extensive work-up on her and found that she's diabetic and has high blood pressure. You know she's had arthritis for years and it's gotten worse; she's overweight and needs to have someone around her to see that she eats properly and gets rid of that weight. She doesn't need *intensive* care but she should not be left alone to take care of herself no matter how much she thinks she is able to take care of herself. So that's how the subject of the nursing home came up. We were only trying to find the very best solution to the problem. "

Tina was quiet for a few moments, trying to sort out the situation in her own mind. Certainly, her mother must have the very best of whatever she needs, medical or otherwise, but she was trying to understand why she could not get the same care in David's house since he's a doctor.

"So, help me understand this. You're a doctor, you're well able to give her all the medical attention she needs at home since she lives with you, but instead of getting medical attention at home you've got to put her in a nursing home, right?"   There was complete silence while she waited for a reply from her brother. Finally, she heard a cough.

"No, that's not the way it is at all. If she stayed with us I would have to hire a live-in nurse to look after her and you know how determined and self-sufficient Mama is, she wouldn't have any part of somebody living with her to do everything for her; she'll feel like we're treating her like a child; she'll have a fit!"

"If she lives with me *I'll* have to hire a live-in nurse to look after her, I can't stay home and do it, so what the hell is the difference?"

David was praying he wouldn't have to tell his sister the rest of the story but he had no other choice. "God Almighty, what a mess this has turned out to be. Looks like I'm damned if I do and damned if I don't," he surmised.

"Well, her health is not the whole issue here. Now, Tina, please try to understand, from my point of view, what I'm going to say, O.K?"

Sarcastically, Tina replied, "Go ahead, I'm listening; but I'm telling you before you begin, it'd better be good."

"Well," David started, "For a long time now Gloria's been complaining about how Mama talks, you know, her bad English and awful diction and stuff ...... "

"All right, now we're getting somewhere. I should've known that bitch you have for a wife had something to do with it. David, are you so naïve that you can't see what Gloria is doing; or is it that you just love her so much you're blinded and can't see? Can't you see what she's trying to do?"

"What're you talking about? You didn't let me finish," David shot back, getting a little annoyed at her attitude.

He probably thought Tina would start screaming and cussing to high heaven, but incredibly, she said in a most disgusted tone,

"O, forget it, David; maybe you can't see what Gloria's up to but I do. All these years Mama's stayed with you, cooked the meals, kept the house, raised your children, with her terrible diction and bad English; neglecting her health, and Gloria let her do it. It seems funny to me that she didn't complain about Mama when she was able to do all the work Gloria should have been paying somebody to do when Mama wasn't as old as she is. In other words, the bad English and the terrible diction didn't mean a damn then, but now that she's old and sick and the children are almost grown, Gloria could care less what happens to Mama or where she goes just as long as she gets the hell out of her house! I bet you' that's what she told you, isn't it?"

"I see it's no use trying to make you understand and I don't have time to argue with you. So, I take it you won't come and get her, right?"

"No, that's NOT right! If she will agree to live with me I'll be on the next plane to pick her up, but *she* will have to tell me that she really wants to do it. My best advice to you is, talk to Mama, tell her I am ready to come and get her if it's what she wants. I am not going to try and persuade her to come with me if she doesn't want to. I just want her to be completely happy for the balance of her life, however long that may be; and I will tell you straight up that I don't appreciate you and that selfish, conniving witch you're married to uprooting her and making her go through these changes at this time in her life. I am not happy with that , not one damn bit!

And by the way, tell me; how come Mama's English and diction are so important to Gloria now? Your children are almost grown and doing very well. If they haven't imitated her bad English and terrible diction by now I'm sure it won't bother them in the future.

Besides, you lived in the house with Mama all your life and when I talk with you I hear perfect English and diction. So, what I'm hearing today is just "crap" ... personified! You call me after you talk to Mama, and remember what I said. I'll be waiting for your call." Without another word she angrily hung up the phone.

Poor David. What could he do now? He was back to square one.

Well, I guess the Bible is still right - 'when I try to do right, evil is present on every hand.' The only thing he could do now is proceed with "Plan A," to find the best nursing home for his mother just in case she refuses to go and live with Tina. The best thing to do would be to turn over the search to his secretary, telling her that the facility must be second to none and as close to where he lived as possible. Money was no object. He told her, "If you find that it's too much for you along with your regular duties, call a temp agency and get someone in here to help; just keep in mind that this matter about my mother is of the utmost importance and expediency!" She promised to give the task her best effort. She was so sad, she really felt sorry for her boss. He was such a good guy. Gazing after him, his shoulders slumped, head bowed in sadness as he left the office on his way to the hospital, the young woman could not help but think, "Gosh! What a guy. His wife is one lucky woman. I hope she realizes it."

With determination the young woman began her assignment. She understood that to accomplish the results her boss expected would be almost miraculous but she was willing to give it "the old college try." The priorities he had set created a block at every call. Nursing Homes, for the most part did not have such a good reputation. Most people believed that nursing homes were for the poor and disenfranchised old people, for people who had no one to care for them. So to find a 'state of the art' one like David wanted was, it appeared, impossible. Nevertheless, determined efforts finally paid off. She found the ideal place called "Elder Living." It had a twenty-four hour on-call highly trained medical staff, tightly gated security, manicured grounds; and if you can believe it, it even had a little cottage with a bedroom, livingroom, fully equipped kitchenette, and bathroom with a shower or Jacuzzi! The facility even allowed the occupants the option to either use its furniture, dishes and cooking utensils or to bring their own things so they would feel comfortable surrounded by their own stuff. It had a security system that operated in conjunction with an arm bracelet to signal help if needed. David was amazed, not only about what the facility offered but he was overwhelmed with the job his secretary had done in such a short time. But the 'icing on the cake' for David was, he would be permitted to provide other amenities that his mother might desire. He knew there would be other things she would want. Old people are like that. They become attached to something and it becomes a part of them, kind of like a baby's "blankey." Maybe that's why some people call it "going back to childhood" - regression. David was sure that his mother's 'blankey' would be her rose beds. But at her age and physical condition she could not handle the task of taking care of a rose garden. How was he to overcome it? Well, it was back to the drawing board.

He went back to his secretary, explaining the situation to her and soliciting – yes, praying for whatever thoughts she might come up with. He certainly had none of his own. It's no wonder that smart secretaries are most often referred to as "my right arm" by their boss; these women should more accurately be called "my private magician;" for they always seem to be ready with a 'rabbit in the hat' in situations that seem impossible. David was distraught, no idea in the world of what to do about it, but to his secretary it was all in a day's work. She leaned back in her comfortable secretary's chair and told him matter-of-factly, "That's no problem, Dr. Mac, we'll hire a gardener He'll do the work, she can do the supervising."

David was thoughtful for a minute, then exclaimed, "That's right. You're right! Why didn't I think of that?"

"Well, you're not the secretary, I am." David leaned across her desk and gave her a kiss on the cheek. The grin on his face spelled relief. That was it. The problem was solved, Thank God!

David left his office early. He had to tell his wife what he had done for his mother, hoping she would agree with it; then he had to break the news to his mother. God knows, that was the hardest thing he ever had to do in all his life. Scholastic tests, exams, board certifications, waiting for results of laboratory tests ..... all were minor compared to facing his mother with his decision to move her out of their home. She had been both mother and father to him for most of his life, and he had wanted more than anything else in the world to make her proud of him, to take care of her. Deep inside he knew she would not be agreeable with this arrangement. Nevertheless, something had to be done. He had no other choice. It was such a painful thing to have to do. The more he thought about moving his mother out of the house, the more condemned he felt in his spirit. He loved his wife, he loved his mother; yet, it seemed impossible to make them happy; the two women in the world that he loved most. He thought he had solved the problem by finding the most elite living accommodations available. That remained to be seen.

For once he got home before Gloria did. Rarely did this happen.

When Gloria arrived he took her into their bedroom where they would be private.

"I found the place for Mama." He waited for her response.

"Well, that certainly was quick. Tell me about it."

David began to tell his wife about the "Elder Village" that his secretary had found. When he had finished describing it, Gloria was thrilled. In fact, she was amazed.

"You see, I knew you could work it out. That's great! Good job! When are you going to tell her?"

"Well, I would tell her tonight but I think I'll wait until tomorrow. I've had a hectic day and I really don't feel like dropping this on her tonight."

" You might as well get it over with. There's no better time like the present, I always say."

"Gloria, look, I am not rushing Mama out of this house. Let's not talk about it anymore, I feel bad enough already."

"Humph! It's your call, baby; just get it done."

When she made that remark David's thoughts went back to Tina's remarks about Gloria. His wife couldn't really be evil like that. That's impossible. "She's my wife, the mother of my children! She loves my mother." Could this be a color from her coat of many colors?"

He decided to wait until tomorrow to talk to his mother. "I'll need all the strength I can muster so I might as well start preparing myself with a good night's rest." He took a nice long warm shower and went to bed dreading the next day's task. It had been a tiring day. He just wanted to blot out everything, pretend it never happened. As if turning off his subconscious mind, he slept peacefully.

Early the next morning, Gloria woke her husband with a kiss. She paused long enough to say a few words of encouragement to him.

"Honey, I can understand how you feel, but it's something that must be done. If I could do it for you, I would. I know you will find the right words to say to your mother and I believe she will go along with the program." She put her arms around him, squeezing him tightly, "Just remember, I love you baby. It'll be alright, you'll see." Hurrying into her jacket and pulling her shoulder bag onto her shoulder, she rushed downstairs, yelling back, "See ya' tonight. Have a good day." He did not reply, his thoughts had immediately turned to the method of approach he would use to talk to his mother this morning. He lay on his back staring at the ceiling reading an imaginary script. But as he rehearsed the dialogue over and over, shame, condemnation and discouragement engulfed him. His mother's sweet loving face, now wrinkled and drooped from age loomed before him as he imagined the look of disbelief it would display when she heard what he would say. Funny, he remembered that look only one other time ... the day his brother Michael rebelled against her and left home. It was a look he always hoped he would never see on her face again. But life sure does play tricks on us sometime for here he was getting ready to do the same thing to her. Something inside him was saying, "Boy, you are one lousy bum! How could you treat your old mother like that?" He shook his head vigorously as though it would make the voice go away, and forced himself to get up and start getting dressed, deciding that the best way to face a problem is head on.

Dressed impeccably in freshly dry-cleaned sharply pressed dark blue trousers, snow white dress shirt and dark blue tie; shoes shining like glass – he was looking good! He slowly walked the distance to Lillie's quarters on the rear of the ground floor. He thought to him, "Death row prisoners walking the 'last mile' to the death chamber couldn't feel any worse than this." Finally he reached the door of Lillie's sitting room, paused a moment, then knocked softly.

"Come on in, whoever it is," he heard his mother say. She was out of bed and dressed as usual, sitting in her favorite chair watching the morning news on television.

"Good morning, Mama," David mustered, his head bowed.

Without moving her eyes from the TV screen she replied, "Good morning, baby. What you doing down here this time o'day? You usually be at the hospital by now, don't you?"

"Yes, maam; I told them I'd be a little late this morning."

"Is sumpn' the matter?"

" Nothing's the matter, I just need to talk to you about something and I want you to listen with an open mind and understand what I'm saying, OK?"

"Um huh, I'll listen with a open mind, I cain't hardly listen with it closed, can I?"

David sighed as if to say, "Let's get this over with." Then like a tirade of unstoppable waves, he blurted out the story of her health and how she needs daily monitoring; how he had found this lovely Elder Village, describing in detail the amenities including the rose garden with her own gardener. He tried with all his might to make it enticing, hoping she would agree to move there without much persuasion.

"But, of course, if it sounds like something you might not be happy with, there is another alternative. I've talked to Tina and she still wants you to come up there and stay with her. It's your choice, whatever you'd rather do. He finished talking and waited for her response. He waited, there was no reply. Lillie was quiet --- too quiet. David was becoming anxious. What was going on in that old head of wisdom and gray hair? What was she thinking? Didn't she understand a word he had said? He decided to break the silence.

"Mama, did you hear what I said?"

Without turning her head to look at him, she continued to stare straight at the television set. "Yeah, I heard what you said." She seemed so undisturbed, so nonchalant, not interested.

"Well, what about it, what do think?" David's heart had begun to pound rapidly, perspiration forming on his forehead. This was more difficult than he had expected. Knowing his mother, he was sure she would have some objection; after all, at her age she could be expected to show some sort of resistance to this sudden change to her lifestyle. He clearly understood that she would not be enthusiastic about the move no matter how pleasant he tried to make it for her. What else could he do?

"What do I think?" Lillie slowly turned her huge body so she would be face to face with her son. "I think you think I'm a bigger fool than I really am. I ain't got a whole lot o' education but I sho' ain't that big a fool! I know what you tryin' to tell me. You tryin' to tell me I ain't no more good for you and yo' family and I got to git outta heah. I know that's what it is. You cain't bring yo'self to come out and say it but I know that's the truth, ain't it? "

"Aw, see there; Mama, you know that's not true! We're not putting you out of here, we'd never do that to you. We love you. That's why I went to such lengths to see that you'll be well cared for by the best medical staff and have everything humanly possible at your disposal to make you comfortable and happy. I wouldn't be doing that if I didn't love you. We're only concerned about your physical health, that's all."

Lillie took a deep breath.

"Well, Son, I heard everything you said but I didn't hear no sign of love in one word. But you know, the Lawd don't let nuthin' slip up on me. I kind o' knowed this would happen some day. In fact, I'm surprised it didn't happen before now. Yo' wife ain't never been happy 'bout me stayin' heah. O' she tried to put on her little act like she loved me; but I felt in my spirit, deep down inside, that someday she would show her true colors, you know, like one o' them lizards that change colors all the time so you never know what they *really* look like. They change and be whatever color they need to be. You know what I mean? Now since y'all's kids done growed up and almost ready to go 'way to college or get married, y'all ain't got no mo' use for me. I guess it's like they say, 'When peoples gits old and cripple or sick, the people they thought loved em' just throws 'em away like a old dishrag. I heard a song one time – I think one of them gospel singing blind boys from Mississippi used to sing it, that said, 'You don't know what you gon' come to before you die.' That's the truth. We really don't know what's gon become of us before we die. But I thank God I know one thing. My Bible tells me,, 'When your mother and your father forsake you, then the Lord will take you up.' So, you can put me out o' your house but the Lawd already got another place for me somewhere. He ain't never let me down before and He ain't gon' let me down now. I know I'm welcome in Tina's and Alvin's home. They been begging me to come up there and stay with them, but it's too cold up there; I ain't never been in no snow and ice. I'm too old now and cain't git 'round like I used to so how I'm gon' make friends up there? Tina and Al is always gone somewhere. I would be lonesome up there, all my friends, folks I knowed all my life is down heah. I love them chilun for wantin' me to come up there but I'll stay heah where I belong. God's got a place for me. You'll see."

David just looked at his mother, without replying. She was illiterate and her English and diction were not as they should be but his mother had a way of making you understand where she was coming from, which made him feel that much more ashamed of what he had told her. Poor David. The 'Apple of his father's eye;' the famous doctor, her son that she had always dreamed of; the son who was going to always take care of his mother and not leave her like the other son did. "What a fool you are," his spirit condemned him.

"Well, anyway, I 've arranged to take you out there tomorrow. I'll take the day off and take you so you can see what you think about the place, OK?"

I'm a stranger, don't drive me away;
I'm a stranger, don't drive me away.
If you drive me away,
You're gonna need my help someday.
I'm a stranger, don't drive me away.

Lillie didn't answer. She had changed her gaze from the television to the window becoming fixated on an unfamiliar car that was moving slowly down the road. It was an older car, not like the cars she was accustomed to seeing in that area. It was common to see expensive sports cars that belonged to the neighbors' teenage kids speeding down the road. She thought, "They must be somebody who done got lost out here in the country and trying to find their way back to town." She was not aware that David had left the room.

She sat motionless in her rocking chair, staring out the window. The sun was shining brightly upon the dark green well-manicured grass; bathed with fresh morning dew the scene reminded her of Christmas lights, dancing, glistening in the morning light. As she looked out on the scenery, she marveled, "What a Great and Mighty God! Only God could create such a beautiful picture." As she thought on the awesomeness of God her mind wandered back over the years of her life, especially the years since her husband died. The road had not been easy; in fact, there were times when the devil had whispered in her ear, "Why don't you just give up, let somebody else raise them chillum. Go out and have a good time like other young women; there's plenty o' men out there who would be glad to git' a woman like you." To which she would simply smile and say, "You git on behind me Satan. I cain't give up now, I done come too far to turn 'round." That was pretty much her theme through the years – not to give up but instead to wait on God. She had that kind of a relationship with God.

She sat there glowing in that mystical feeling when suddenly there was a knock on the door. She looked around expecting David to answer the knock but he was not in the room. She did not realize that he had left; she was so caught up in her thoughts. "Who is that?" she called out.

"It's me, Mama, can I come in?" David asked.

"Yeah, child, you can come on in. The door ain't locked."

The door slowly opened just enough for David to poke his head inside. "There's somebody here to see you, Mama," David stepped back and the door opened wide. In the doorway, his head almost touching the top of the door stood a tall handsome young man. He spoke the words that for 20 years she had prayed to hear. "Hey Mama; it's Michael."

Lillie turned the chair in the direction of the voice. She studied the figure in the doorway, hoping that her eyes were not playing tricks on her. After a few moments it dawned on her that what she had been praying for all these years was standing in that doorway!

"Michael!" " O' my God, it's my baby! He done come home!! My child done come home!

> *He's an on time God, Yes He is;*
>
> *He's an on time God, Yes He is;*
>
> *He may not come when you want Him,*
>
> *But He'll be there on time.*
>
> *He's an on time God, Yes He is.*

Lillie struggled to get out of her chair but Michael hurriedly came to her rescue. Kneeling in front of her, he lowered his head onto her lap his arms stretching to encircle her body --- he wept. Lillie was crying while at the same time whispering over and over, "Thank You, Jesus; Thank You, Jesus; Thank You, Jesus."

They looked like they were glued together. Neither of them was willing to let the other go. This was the day Lillie had spent 20 plus years praying for and she didn't want to end it. She could now earnestly understand how the father of the prodigal son in the story in the Bible must have felt when his son came back home. The feeling was indescribable!

When mother and son finally released their hold on each other, they just stared at each other for a few moments; then with tears of unspeakable joy welling up in their eyes, they hugged again.

Michael positioned himself on the floor in front of his mother, sitting Indian-style. He almost felt ashamed to speak but he forced himself to do so.

"Mama, I know I'm unworthy of your forgiveness. There is no excuse for what I've done to you, leaving home the way I did and not letting you know where I was or what I was doing. There is just no reason for it, no excuse for it except that I was young and foolish.

Knowing the kind of mother you are, I know how worried and concerned you had to be. Nobody has to tell me, I know that I put you through many years of heartache and I am truly sorry. Can you ever forgive me?"

"I forgave you the same night you left home, baby. I never did hold it against you for leaving home. I knowed you were just like you said, young and foolish. I just prayed and asked God to forgive you, to take care o' you and bring you back home someday. "

"Well, I can tell you that I knew you were praying for me because I got into some things in my young life that I was supposed to spend a lot of time in jail for, but the Lord brought me out. And there were a few times when I could have lost my life but the Lord stepped in and saved me. That's why I know *you* were praying for me, nobody else was. And I just want to tell you now that I thank you for believing in me in spite of my disobedience and rebellion. But most of all, I thank you for having faith in God and for keeping me constantly before Him in prayer. Ever since I gave my life to Christ, I realized what a blessing it is to have a good mother to pray for you. I really wish that everybody knew that."

"Honey, you say you gave your life to Christ?" Lillie was wondering if she really heard what she thought she'd heard.

"That's right, Mama." He stood up, put his hands in his pockets and turned his back to his mother, ashamed to face her and say what he was going to say next. "I had been claiming I was a Christian but I wasn't until a few years ago. I had been just *playing* with God, playing church. You know how some people go to church every Sunday and shout and throw their hands up in the air acting like they're praising the Lord, then after they leave the church they do the same things sinners do or something worse? Well, that's more or less what I was doing; that is, until one night when I was watching an Oral Roberts program on TV. A lot of people were testifying about what God had done in their lives. Oral Roberts himself talked about how because of his mother's prayers and his sister's prayers, the Lord healed him of tuberculosis. That was an incurable disease in those days. A lot of people died from it. He also talked about how rebellious and hardheaded he was as a young man until the Lord saved him and set him on the right road. I was condemned in my spirit, thinking about my own life; so I fell on my knees and asked the Lord to forgive me, to cleanse me of my unrighteousness, come into my life, change me, and make me a new creature.

> *The Potter saw a vessel,*
> *that had been broken by the wind*
> *and the rain;*
> *And He sought with so much compassion,*
> *To put it together again.*
> *Well, I was that broken vessel,*
> *That everyone thought was no good;*
>
> *But Jesus picked up the pieces,*
> *And made me whole again.*
> *Jesus picked up the pieces*
> *Of my broken life, my broken life, one day.*
> *He made me a new vessel*
> *And revived my soul again.*

Lillie sat anxiously watching her son, noting the intenseness of his face. Her heart was beating so fast she thought it would jump right out of her chest! Listening to her long lost son's confession of his conversion, she realized that not only had God brought her son back home, He had brought him back to her *a changed man – just like she had asked Him to do!* The son that left home years ago, preparing himself for a life on the other side of the law, had come back home a Christian on the side of the Lord. What a Mighty God we serve! It took a few minutes for both of them to recover from the moment, for the Holy Spirit was in the room. There was a lot of "Hallelujah" and "Thank You Jesus" in the air!

"I'm so glad to know you're a Christian, honey; that sho' is good news. I want to hear all about what happened to you after you left; you was just 17 years old, you know. But let me git' up from heah and make you something to eat. I know you're hungry, ain't you?"

"I didn't have breakfast yet but I'm not really hungry. Seeing you, being here with you, I guess it took my appetite. I didn't expect to see all this, I mean, how David has prospered. Looks like he really did well for himself."

"Yeah, he did. He always said he was gon' be a doctor and make lots o' money, and he did."

"We talked a little bit when I first got here. I couldn't believe that was him that opened the door for me! I know it's been a long time but I remember him as a little skinny quiet boy with his head in a book all the time."

Lillie laughed at the thought. "Yeah, he sure was skinny and was readin' some kind o' book all the time. Always talking 'bout he was gon' be a doctor. He did good. He's been a good boy. He just works too hard, I think. His wife works, too. Both of 'em makes good money and they's living a good life."

"Yeah buddy; I can tell that they're doing alright for themselves! This house, alone, is evidence of that! I didn't see his wife and he didn't say anything about her. I guess he knew I wanted to see you, so he brought me back here. Where does his wife work?"

"O , she's a school teacher but she don't teach no more. She's on the Education Board or sumpn' and got a office downtown. "

"O yeah? Gosh! I guess my little brother has truly been blessed. Well, I'm happy for him. I didn't see any children, do they have any?"

Lillie's eyes lit up. "Do they have any? Child, they got four o' them things." She reared her head back and laughed one of those proud grandparent 's laughs. Mike, can you believe it? I got myself four grandchilun. David was just getting ready to go to high school when you left, now he got a boy ready to graduate from high school. Ain't that sumthin'?"

Michael agreed and laughed with her. "It sure is."

Michael was thoughtful for a moment, then, "By the way, where is Tina and what is she doing? Is she married, got any children?"

"Tina's living in New York. She married a very nice young man. They own a record company and they fly all over the country, even overseas; but they haven't got no chiluns yet. You know Tina, she ain't never wanted no chillum, and I think her husband just wants whatever she wants. He sho' is a good boy. He gives her anything she wants. When they got married he made her vice-president of his record company!." Michael was impressed.

"My goodness, that is really something! I'm so glad to hear that. I'd really like to see Tina. My only little sister. "

"I got her telephone number, you can call her if you want to."

"That would be great,"

"Look over there on the table 'side o' my bed and you'll see a address book. Look in there and you'll see her phone number."

Michael did as his mother instructed him but did not see the number. "How is it listed in here by her first name or last name?"

"It just say 'Christina,' you just have to look until you see it. Just keep looking, it's in there." Michael turned several pages until he saw "Christina."

"Here it is. I found it Mama. Is it OK if I call her now?

"Why sho', baby, you go right ahead and talk to yo' sister as long as you want to. She gon' be so glad to heah yo' voice."

Michael dialed the number, it rang several times then an answering machine came on with a message: "You have reached the home of Al and Christina Joyner. We are not available to take your call at the moment. If your call is regarding business, please call our offices at 452-2226. If this is a personal call, please clearly speak your name and phone number, and leave a brief message if you'd like. We will get back to you as soon as possible. Thank you."

"Well, I reached their answering machine. I didn't leave no message. I'll try again later."

"She say when she see my phone number on her ID machine, she know I don' called so she calls me back. So she might call back before you call her again. When she find out you're heah she'll prob'ly get a plane and come down heah! Tina is so crazy. I will never understand how Al gave her a position in his company like that. Must be just 'cause he loves her so much, cause Tina ain't never been known to have a job sittin' behind a desk. She have to be on the go all the time. Maybe he just wanted her to be wit' him. Whatever it was, I'm glad she found a good man like that. He sure is good to her, worships her. What about you, baby, you got a wife and chiluns?" she asked expectantly.

"No, maam; neither one of those. I've never been married; "and," he told her sheepishly, "as far as I know I don't have any children. But I still have time and as soon as I find the right girl I'll get married."

"You mean to tell me you ain't got married in all these years you been gone?"

"No, maam, I didn't."

"Well what you been doing? Come on, I wanta heah 'bout yo' life; what's been happening to you? I wanna heah all about everything."

"Well, I remember the day I left home like it was yesterday. I stayed with some of my "partners in crime" you might call them, for a while. Then we decided to go to California. One of the guys had an old car and, to show you how foolish we were, we believed that old run down car would get us from Georgia to California. Shucks, the thing wasn't good enough to get us to Alabama let alone to California! But we were sure it would, so we struck out in it. It got us about 60 miles down the road then started smoking and the brakes went out. So we got out, left the car on the side of the road and started hitchhiking. Luckily, hitchhiking back then was not as dangerous as it is now. I wouldn't hitchhike to the house next door these days!." He and Lillie both laughed at that. "Any how, I don't understand how we made it but we did. Somehow, we got to California – and in one piece, too. We, naturally, hooked up with our kind of people. It's funny how they know one another without being introduced. We got our thing going, making good money doing things we should not be doing. Every once in a while, we would get picked up by the law for a misdemeanor ....."

"Mis-da- meanor? What in the world is that?" Lillie wanted to know.

"A misdemeanor is something you do that's against the law but it's what they call a 'minor offense.' So they don't give you a lot of time or a jail sentence for it. Sometime it's just a day or two in jail or the judge will make you pay a fine or something like that."

"O... OK. I see what you mean. I see that on the television sometime, they be talking 'bout somebody had to pay a fine for something like that."

"That's right. So, I was picked up several times and put in jail but I never had to serve time. And, it's the funniest thing, Mama, every time I would be picked up I'd have to stay overnight and go to court the next morning and every time I went to court, I went before the same judge. There were plenty of other judges but I got the same judge every single time. Can you believe that? Well, anyhow, I never will forget the last time I went before him --- I don't remember his name --- after the clerk read the charges against me, the judge took his glasses off and leaned over on the bench. He looked me squarely and disgustedly in my face. 'Young man, every time I turn around you're in my court. I'm tired of seeing your ugly face in my courtroom.' He leaned back in his chair, that disgusted stare still on his face, ' so I'm going to do you and your family a big favor. Have you registered for the Selective Service, young man?' I started to tell a lie and say 'yes' but I knew he could very easily find out the truth, so I told him I had not registered. He called the Sheriff and told him, 'Take this young man to the post office, get him registered for the Selective Service, then take him to the Army Recruiting Office and have them take him in the military.' Young man, you heard what I just said. Now, you have a choice, you can either go into the military or I can give you a sentence for prison where I promise you, you won't like it very much. Which will it be, prison or the army? You choose." When I heard 'prison sentence' it only took me a second to choose between jail and the army." He burst out laughing, Lillie joined him.

"I understand what you mean, baby. So you went into the army?"

"Yes, maam. I was scared to death but I went on in. I can truly tell you that the military is where you separate the boys from the men.

You might be a boy when you go in but I guarantee you, you will be a man when they get through with you." He smiled authoritatively at his mother.

"How long did you stay in the army?" Lillie wanted to know.

"Well, let me finish the story. If you remember, I was always the big man, my "boys" took orders from me, and I didn't take orders from nobody. When I went into the army, those sergeants let me know right away that they gave the orders, not me. They cut me down to size *real* quick! They were good to me, they didn't take advantage of me or treat me bad they just made a man out of me. They taught me responsibility, moral responsibility; to be true to my fellow servicemen and myself. Mama, those older guys – and there were some, especially the drill sergeants, that had been in the military for 20 years. They loved it and didn't want to get out. They took me under their wing and would not give up on me. They used to make me talk about my home life and how I had been raised; how I rebelled and left home, the trouble I had gotten myself into and I left home and how the judge had made me go into the army rather than give me a jail sentence. They told me that was nothing but the Lord taking care of me. And they told me something I already knew, that I was blessed because I had a Christian mother back home that was praying for me. Those older guys never let me forget that. Not that I would have forgotten you, you're my mother; but they made me understand how blessed I was to have a mother like you, and for that I will always be grateful to them."

"Hallelujah! Thank You, Lord," Lillie almost shouted.

"So you see, I found a home in the army. I was well taken care of. I had to work hard – like real men do, I guess – but I was paid for it and my mentors were always available to help me if I had a problem. Mama, sometime they treated me like daddy used to treat me. They didn't baby me. They would often tell me, 'You got to learn how to roll with the punches, boy; life is full of bumps, and knocks, and bruises, so you got to be tough. Don't be a bully or be mean, but be tough. ' One of our presidents – I think it was Teddy Roosevelt – said, 'Walk softly but carry a big stick.' I think that's what they meant. I guess they must've seen something in me that nobody else had seen, other than you." He looked over at his mother and smiled lovingly.

"If I said it once I said it a thousand times: I don' care how bad a child is, a real mother will see some good in him. That ain't no bad thing, a mother ought to love her child no matter what he do. That don't mean they like what the child is doing, but they love the child."

"I see what you mean. Anyway, there was this older guy. He had been in the army about 30 years. He was a first sergeant, everybody respected him; he was kind of like a father to us younger guys and a big brother to the older guys. His wife died of cancer and they didn't have any children so the army was all he had. He would always tell me, 'Mike, don't just while away your life, do something worthwhile with your life. You're young now but if you keep on living you'll be old someday and you'll look around and you won't have anything to show for all those years you've lived. So do something constructive with your life while it's still time.' One day he asked me, 'Mike, with all the opportunities the army is offering, how come you haven't taken advantage of some of them?' I asked him what he meant and he said, 'How come you haven't finished school, got your GED? I know you went through the 11th grade, it wouldn't take you long to finish that last year and get your GED. After that, it's no telling how far you could go.' Well, I thought about it and decided to take his advice. I got my GED and seem like it just whetted up my appetite for education. I started working on my Associates Degree in Sociology. " He watched his mother, waiting for her anxious response. She was leaning forward in her chair, eyes stretched wide, mouth open wide.

"So, did you ever git yo' degree?" as if she had her fingers crossed and praying for a positive answer. He hesitated for a minute, teasing her.

"Well----------, Of course I got my degree, what do you think?" Going over and giving her a big hug.

"O, my baby, I'm so proud o' you and what you done with your life. I thank God for that man and all them other army men who took you like their own son. It was the hand of God; it was God takin' care o' you like I asked Him to. Ain't God a good God?"

"All the time," Michael answered, "And all the time He is good."

"So then, how long did you stay in the army? You still in there?"

"No, maam; I stayed in 16 years then I decided to get out and see what civilian life was like. See, with my associates degree, I knew I wouldn't have any trouble getting a job. I remembered what you told me the day I left home, about how things would be different for Blacks by the time I got grown, that doors of opportunity would be opening for us. Sure enough, I found a job at the Halfway House in town, counseling the same kind of guys I left home with many years ago. Isn't that ironic? Like the 'sarge' used to say, 'Life sure is strange.' But I like it. I feel like I'm doing something "constructive," as the 'sarge' used to say. Some day I plan to go back to school and get a degree in psychology."

"O' my God, heah we go again; we gon' have another doctor in the family!" She roared, laughing so loud you could hear her outside. Michael was happy that he had made his mother happy. He had prayed that his homecoming and the knowledge of what he had done with his life in a positive way, would in some small way compensate for the worry he had put her through.

There was still one thing she was dying to know. "Honey, why didn't you ever call or write in all them years you wuz' gone? Why didn't you tell us you wuz' in the army? All of us nearly worried ourself to death!"

"I didn't contact you at first because I was still arrogant and rebellious and I just knew I could make it on my own. I wanted to prove to everybody that I was a man. But, like I told you, it ended when the good judge put me in the army. After I got in there and began to straighten out my life, I felt so guilty and ashamed, I just couldn't bring myself to call you. I decided that I couldn't or wouldn't come home and look you in the face until you could see the "new and improved" son , not the one that stormed out of your house more than 20 years ago. Remember the sergeant I told you about, the one whose wife died with cancer and he had no children? Well, he retired, and after he was gone I realized it was time to come back. I got out after I finished my last three years that I'd signed up for and came home. I went into the Army Reserves just in case I couldn't make it in civilian life. I went to where our house used to be. Nobody was around that I remembered, everything was so unfamiliar. I got a phone book and began to look for David. I remembered that he always swore he would be a doctor someday and after I found my job, that's how I found him ----- and of course, you. " Lillie had listened intently.

Then a sadness came over her face. Her mind went back to David's conversation with her earlier that day. "Well, I guess it's a good thing you came home when you did or you might not've found me heah", she told him.

"You said I might not've found you here? Why not, are you moving?"

"Well, according to your brother he's moving me out and into a nursing home."

"A nursing home? Are you kidding me? Why would he put you in a nursing home? Mama, you must not've heard him correctly, I'm sure David didn't say that!"

"Yeah, he did. He said it this morning just befo' you got heah."

"You look pretty healthy to me; what would he put you in a nursing home for? I don't get it."

"I don't think it's David's idea. I think it's his wife's idea. She ain't never really wanted me heah. You see, when they wuz young and just startin' out and didn't have nothing she put on her acting shows pretending she loved me so; but I knowed deep in my heart that she just wanted me around to take care o' the chillum, cook and clean the house, so she would have the time she needed to git her college degrees and make a whole lot o' money. Every now and then she would say somethin' to hurt my feelings; but I never said nothin' to David 'bout it cause he was working so hard, I didn't want him to have to worry 'bout it. I found out a few days ago, I got dibetes and high blood pressure and arth-ritis all over my body. I don' have to take the insulin every day, I have to take pills. So, I ain't disable, I can still cook for myself, I can bathe myself and I can still do most of the things I always done; but the doctor don't want me to do a whole lots o' things like digging in my rose bed, and cleaning the house and stuff like that. But I guess David's wife don't want me 'round no more so he found this place that he say is not really a nursing home, they call it Elder Living or Elder Village or sumpn' like that."

Michael was shocked! "He didn't say a word about it this morning. When is this supposed to take place?"

"Well, the last thing I heard him say is, 'I'll take tomorrow off and take you out there to see it.' I ain't seen the place so I don't know what it looks like or anything. He say it's very, I guess you would call it, "ritzy" and all that. I got the feeling he was trying to make up for moving me out. But he don't have to do that cause I believe God already have a place prepared for me, and I don't mean a place in heaven, neither - at least not right now. He's got a place prepared for me right down heah'. Tina's been beggin' me for years to come and stay with her and I love the child for wantin' me there.

Her and her husband, they's so sweet. But you see, I ain't never been no where but in the south and it's too cold up there where they live in all that snow and ice. I'm too old for that now."

Michael was reflective for a few moments, a million questions swirling around in his head as he tried to put the pieces of this puzzle together.

"You said it 's a place called Elder Living or Elder Village?"

"Yeah, that's right. You ever heard of 'em?"

"Yes, maam, I have. It's a new thing they're doing for elderly people if they can afford it. I've never seen one but I hear they are really 'state of the art' places with everything a wealthy person could ever want; and the medical care is superb, so I hear."

"Well, I don't care what they have in 'em, they ain't got my grandchiluns in there." Mike got it! He now understood her feelings.

"So, it's not that you mind moving, you just don't want to leave your grandchildren, is that it?" Michael waited patiently for her answer as she tried to find the words to describe her feelings.

"Natcha'ly, I would miss David and this house. That's all I've had since you left home and Tina left home. David and his family was all I had; so, sho' I'll miss 'em. But I will miss seeing my grandchilun grow up. I been wit 'em all they life, ever since they come into this world I been wit 'em. I'll miss 'em," Her eyes began to tear up. Watching his mother, now old, face wrinkled, carrying too much weight. When she had struggled to rise from a sitting position he noticed it was painful for her, arthritis was really showing its ugly face. She was still her independent self, however; for at those times when he went to her to help, she immediately shooed him away telling him, "No, no, baby, that's alright, I can make it." And she did make it by herself. He understood then why she was resistant to leaving this place. "You are devoted to those kids, aren't you?" There was no hesitation. " Child, you don't know how much I love them younguns'. I don't know what I woulda done all these years if it hadn' a been for them. They helped me to live. Whenever I would tell 'em. I'm old, them chillum would tell me, 'Granny, you're not old, you're sweet and well-preserved.' And the baby would jump up on my lap, put her arms 'round my neck and say, 'Granny, you're my best friend. I love you this-s-s-s-s-s-s-s-s- much!' She would stretch her little arms out as wide as she could to show me how much "this"was." Throwing her head back and laughing, slapping her thigh, Mike could see how special those kids were to her " That baby was really sumpn', I tell you. And since the oldest ones have got older and in their teens, they never fail to come back heah' and ask if they can do anything for Granny befo' they leave for school or befo' they go to bed. How can I not miss them? They's my grandchiluns!"

"I see what you're getting at, Mama. Where is the place he's talking about, is it near here?"

"I think he said it's not far from here. I don't remember all he said cause I just shut him out. I was so hurt when he said it. My mind went back to the years he was in high school, planning to be a doctor and I was so proud of him. I had so many hopes and dreams for that boy. "

"Ha!Ha!Ha!Ha!Ha!Ha!Ha!Ha!Ha!Ha!Ha!

See there old woman; you had 'so many

hopes and dreams for that boy.' 'My son gon' be a doctor, make lots o' money, take care o' his mama. ' Yeah, Right! Look what the doctor's doing to his Mama! He's kicking yo' black behind out. He don't need you no more. Ha!Ha!Ha!Ha!Ha!Ha!Ha!Ha!Ha!Ha! "

The devil laughed in her ear. Michael watched as his mother's face seemed to age more right before him. She was devastated because of David's intention to move her out of his house, the place she had called home for so many years. She hadn't showed any emotion about it because, to tell the truth she was in sort of denial. She heard David give the long description of the place but when the realization hit her that he was really putting her out of her home

she emotionally closed her ears the way people do when what they're hearing hurts too much, putting themselves into denial. He walked over to her chair, took a handkerchief from his pocket and pressed it into her hand. As she dabbed at her tear-filled eyes, Michael cleared his throat and told her, "Mama, come with me to the window for a minute." He assisted her in rising. She didn't resist this time. It seemed like talking about her life and what her life had come to made her too tired to get up by herself. "Stay here at the chair for a minute, Mama" He walked to the window, peering out.

"It's not there. Do you feel like walking to the front of the house? I want to show you something."

"Sho', I can walk to the front door." Together they slowly walked from Lillie's quarters on the rear of the house to the front door.

When they reached the door, Michael opened the door and pointed to a black sedan that was five years old and parked in front of the house. "See that old car sitting there, Mama? That's my car." Lillie's eyes widened, she sucked her breath in and replied in disbelief, "That's the car I saw this morning when David was in my room talking to me. I watched it, driving up and down the road. Was that you?"

"Yep; that was me. I had been driving for a while trying to find this place. I got up early this morning determined to find my mother before the sun goes down."

"Well son, all I can say is, I am so happy that you had that determination. You will never know how happy I am that you're home. It was nothing but the Holy Spirit that led you to come home on this particular day and at this particular time. God sho' is good!"

"Yes, maam, He sure is. But the reason I brought you to the door to see my car is this; you can easily see that it is not like David's fancy cars that you're used to seeing ...."

"That's alright ----- " Lillie started, but Michael stopped her.

"Sh–h-h-h-h," he calmly instructed her. "Look around this room, this fabulous house and grounds. I have a job but I can't afford anything like this. All I have is a one-bedroom apartment; but what I'm trying to say is, if you don't mind living in my small apartment with me until I can find a larger one, of course, come on and go home with me. You can have the bedroom and I'll sleep on the couch. In that way, you will be close to your grandchildren that you love so much and you'll still be with family ---- me! How about it?"

"O my God, baby, do you mean it? I don't have to go to that nursing home?"

"Of course not! No mother of mine is going to a nursing home if I can help it. Besides, you don't belong in no nursing home – I don't care if they do call it an Elder Village, I don't care how ritzy and state-of-the-art it is. I'm sure David thinks he's doing the right thing, and I'm just as sure that he loves you. It's just that – if I understand correctly – he's got a demanding, manipulating and domineering wife and apparently she's running the show. Ill tell you straight up, I wouldn't want to be in his shoes, having to choose between my wife and my mother. That must really be a trip, boy!"

"I guess you right, son. Po' child. Like my daddy used to say, 'You make yo' bed hard you have to lie in it.' I'm just glad the Lawd sent you by heah so you can take me off'n his hands so he can be rid of one of his problem. Ain't that right?"

"Yes, maam. I'm happy about that, too. So that means you don't mind living with me and sharing the little bit that I have?"

"No, baby, I don't mind. I'll be happy to go home with you. I believe that's the way God planned it."

> *"Everything that happened to me*
> *that was good, God did it.*
> *Everything that happened to me*
> *That was good, God did it.*
> *Yes, He did.*
> *When I was lost out in a world of sin,*
> *Jesus came and took me in.*
> *Everything that happened to me*
> *That was good, God did it."*

The two of them walked back to Lillie's quarters knowing that they were about to embark upon a new beginning, a new journey for both of them. Lillie was his biological mother but they had lived apart for many years in different environments and leading very different lives. It would take a lot of getting to know one another again; but love would see them through. It was an unspoken mutual faith.

Time sure does fly when you're having fun! Mother and son spent almost the entire day talking, still there was so much more to talk about. Michael wanted to know all about David's marriage, his wife and their children. "Gloria got pregnant wit' David, Jr. when they was in college and they got married and didn't tell me nothin' 'bout it until they graduated. David had to do his internin' and wasn't makin' hardly any money much so he asked me if they could stay in the house wit' me 'til he finished. He was internin' in a hospital about a hundred miles from heah' and come home on the weekend. I never charged 'em anything to stay wit' me. She got a job teaching in the same school where y'all went to school, even tho' she was pregnant. After the baby came she went back to work. Somebody had to keep the baby so I quit working for the Thompsons so I could be home and take care o' him. By the time David finished his intern she was pregnant again with Jolita. She went back to work and I was home to take care of both o' my grandchilluns. I had both of 'em all to myself!" She threw her head back and laughed loudly about that. She seemed to be saying, *"Ye laughs best who laughs last."* As if to say, "I had the last laugh." Michael smiled, "I understand what you're saying." "Yeah, thas' how I got so close to them chillun and got to love 'em so much. I never did get a chance to love David, Jr. the way I wanted to when he was a baby 'cause his momma was so possessive. She didn't want nobody to hold him; she would say, 'You can hold him after while.' One minute she was all sweet and lovey-dovey wit' people and the next minute she act like she the Queen o' Sheba! I never did like people like that. I love 'em but I sho' don't like 'em." Michael didn't quite know what to make of his mother's statement.

"Would you run that one by me again, Mama? I didn't quite get what you mean by you love them but you don't like them."

"Well, it just mean that some people got such a nasty attitude til it's hard to love 'em like the Lawd want us to love 'em; no matter how much faith you have and no matter how much you love the Lawd and try to keep His Commandments. Everybody got feelin's and people can say things that's so hurtful they'll make you cry. But the Lawd commanded us to *love* 'em , He didn't say *like* 'em. I know you sayin' 'How you gon' love somebody and not like 'em at the same time?' Well, look at it like this. God didn't *like* the world, He *loved* it; thas' how come He sent His only Son to give His life on the cross for us, to redeem the world. It was because He *loved* us and not because He *liked* us. He didn't *like the world being sinful* but *He still loved the world.* Now, do you understand what I'm talkin' 'bout?" Michael was amazed! He'd been reading the Bible a lot since he gave his life to Christ, he knew what the Bible says about loving the Lord, loving your neighbor, loving your enemies, forgiving and all that, but as far as he knew it really doesn't say anything about liking anybody.

"Where is that in the Bible?"

"Well, it don't come out and say it like I just said it. You see, when you read the Bible you have to ask the Holy Spirit to give you the understanding and thas' the understanding He gave me. Some people just read the Bible and the real meaning of the Word go right on over their head. All you got to do is read Mark 12:30 and

and you'll see that it don't say nothing about liking nobody. Jesus said to love the Lawd first then love yo' neighbor as yo'self. Ask yo'self, do you like everything you have ever done to yo'self?"

"No, maam; I sure do not!"

"But you didn't stop *loving* yo'self, you just didn't like what you did, ain't that right?"

"Well, yes maam, when you put it like that, I guess, you're right. Yeah, I see what you mean. Just like I didn't stop loving myself when I did something crazy. I hated myself for doing it because it was stupid; but I didn't kill myself or stop loving myself, I sure didn't like myself though. The Lord wants us to keep on loving others even when they do something crazy, but you don't have to *like* what they did. Man, that's rich! You're supposed to hate the bad things people do but at the same time, love the person."

"That's right, honey. And you know what, that go for them men that call they' self loving one another like a man and a woman love each other and them women that call they' self loving each other like a man and a woman love each other, too. God don't want us to hate 'em because He created them just like He created us. See, God loves the sinner, He just hates the sin; He loves the sinner, He don't like the sin. Ain't that right?" Michael was so impressed with his mother's explanation.

"Gosh, Mama, I didn't know you could preach like that!" He laughed, teasing her, but she seriously replied, "I don't call myself no preacher, but anytime you telling the good news about our Lawd and Savior Jesus Christ, that's preaching.!" She raised her hands to the sky and shouted, Hallelujah!

Michael wrote a note and taped it to the door of Lillie's living quarters telling David that it was their mother's wish that she be moved into his apartment. He included his address and phone number in case he wanted to call. Also in the note he included, "I think Mama wants to explain to her grandchildren herself why she is moving out so they won't be hurt too much. So please have David, Jr., and Jolita call so she can talk to them. I will get back to you soon. It was great seeing you again." He put the two suitcases into the car, got his mother comfortable in it and started down the road toward the town he had grown up in. This time, however, he vowed it would be different, for he planned to make up to his mother for all the years she had worried and wondered about him.

"Mama, I guess I'd better explain one thing to you. When I got out of the army I went into the Army Reserves and sometime I'll have to go to camp for a weekend to keep in shape. It'll just be for the weekend, though, so maybe David, Jr. or Jo...., what is her name?"

"You talkin' about my granddaughter, Jolita?"

"Yeah, that's her name. Tell me, why did they name her Jolita? I never heard that name before. It's a pretty name but I just never heard it before. Where did they get it from?"

"They wuz tryin' to give her part o' yo' daddy's name, part o' my name and part o' Tina's name. J-o for your daddy's name, Joe; l-i for part o' my name, Lillie; and t-a for the first and last letters in Tina's name. I wuz real proud o' them for doing that. They named one for you, too. The baby girl's name is Michala. They said that was as close to yo' name as they could get. They call her "Mickey." She laughed.

"Wow! That is so sweet. Whose idea was that?

"Don't ask me cause I don't know. It sounds like something that David would do, not his wife. But I was glad they did it."

"Yeah, I got'cha. That was really nice of them and creative, too. They have four children, right?"

"Um hum; the other boy that's next to Mickey, the baby, his name is Richard and we call him "Ricky." He's a sweet boy; he's the quietest one of 'em. He gon' prob'ly be like his daddy, studyin' all the time."

"Well, I'm glad that David's studying paid off for him. He deserves it. As for his wife, I remember what you used to tell us when we were growing up: 'I'll do anything in the world for you but the one thing I cain't do is marry you. You have to do that for yourself, right or wrong.' That's true, too."

"All o' us have to learn life for ourself, and we all have to make our own mistakes; thas how we grow, by our experiences."

"I know that's right! Mama, you are such a good teacher and a wonderful mother. I'm glad you're *my* mother!"

"Thank you, son. You don't know how long I've waited to hear them words come from yo' lips."

Michael got his mother as comfortable as possible in his small apartment. Just as she had predicted, David, Jr. and Jolita packed up all her personal things and brought them to her. The neighbors' heads sure did turn when two expensive cars parked in front of Michael's apartment house. David, Jr. and Jolita each had their own cars. Immediately, Michael started searching for larger, more modern facilities for his mother and himself. He knew exactly what he wanted, not so much for himself, but for his elderly mother. He inquired of several realtors and soon found a house to buy in the neighborhood he liked, on a street that was quiet with very little traffic and a church nearby. The master bedroom had a full bath and there were no steps for her to climb. The front yard was not very large but it was large enough for a rose garden. Lillie was so easy-going, so easy to please, he knew she would agree with the house that he got for her, but he wanted it to be the best that he could afford, barring none. Nothing lavish like his brother David could afford, but it would be from the heart. He rushed home and told his mother, "Mama, drop what you're doing and get your purse, I want to take you to see something." She didn't question him, she did as he instructed her. They got into the car and drove to the other side of town, close to where they had lived before, where Mike and his siblings grew up. The area had changed a lot, many things that she remembered from the time she lived there were no longer there. The church was still there, though, and she was thrilled to see the old building. Old and in dire need of repairs and paint, it still stood. Sadly, the pastor she knew had gone to be with the Lord several years earlier . She had heard about his death but did not attend his funeral. A lot of demolition and reconstruction had gone on in the neighborhood, new streets were there and some renamed streets, but the church was still there. The neighborhood was beautiful. Michael showed her through a lovely three-bedroom, two-bath brick ranch-style house with a living room, dining room, den, electric kitchen and laundry room with washer and dryer, and a two-car garage; central air and heat and wall-to-wall carpets. Most of all, she would never have to climb any steps!

"So, what do you think?" he asked. She was so overwhelmed, all she could say was, "Beautiful, beautiful, beautiful."

"Do you think you'd like to live in it?"

"Of course I would, but the rent on a house like this must be sky high!"

Michael put his arm around her shoulder. "Sweetheart, we won't be renting it, we're buying it if you like it. So, what's it gonna be, do we take it or not?"

"I say we gon' take it. What you think?"

"I think we're about to become homeowners!" He gave her a big bear hug and they laughed happily -- they were happy!

"Thank You, Jesus! Honey, I never thought you had money 'nuff to buy a house like this."

"Compliments of the U. S. Government. I used my G.I. Benefits. All that time in the army is paying off. Come on, let's get over to the realtor's office and get this show on the road, OK?"

Due to prior business commitments Tina had not been able to come and see Michael right away but they talked on the phone incessantly almost every day, reminiscing about the past; where he had been; what the two of them had been doing all the years he was gone and, of course, she was keeping track of what he and their mother were doing since they reunited. It was so incredible the way things happened, the way Michael showed up right on time and saved their mother from a life in a nursing home. Talking about a real life miracle! This mother who refused to give up on her son and this son who determined that he would not let her see him again until he was a changed person had fulfilled their dreams. Now they only needed to live comfortably enjoying each other, making up for all the years they had lost. As soon as she could, Tina flew down to see her brother. She could only stay for a few days. They spent most of the time talking about the times – past, present and future. It was so funny, Michael remembered Tina as the "Princess." Tina remembered him as "BMOC" – Big Man On Campus. She informed him, "You're still Big Man On Campus in my book, Big Guy." It was such a joy for Lillie to see those two laughing and joking with each other like they did when they were growing up. O' - they all fussed and fought with each other when they were children; but now they were all grown up, with careers, living respectable lives. Truth be told, that's about all a parent can hope for his or her children. Lillie was so thankful that she never had to visit one of her children in jail. That, in it, was a blessing.

-

Very soon Michael and Lillie took up residence in their new home.

Michael, with Lillie's instructions, planted roses for her. They took up membership in the church on the corner from the house and became active in Sunday School and Bible Study Class. Soon Michael was promoted to Director of the Halfway House where he was counselor and he started checking out the curriculums at the nearby colleges, planning to go back to school for his BA Degree. Lillie continued to keep her appointments with her doctor, David's friend. David called often but seldom came to visit, but David, Jr. and Jolita came often and brought the younger children to see her. They would come on Saturday morning and stay all day. It was such a joy to see them, but it was painful to see them leave her house and go home. The little guys would wrap their arms around her neck and ask sadly, "Granny, when are you coming back home?"

"Sweetheart, this heah is Granny's home now. But you know this one thing, you can always come and live with Granny any time you want to and for as long as you want to, you heah? And you always remember, Granny loves, loves, loves my babies!"

The children would cry and cling to their grandmother, "Granny, I love you, I want to stay with you!!" Lillie's heart would melt like butter, no matter how often the scene would occur. She would try as best she could to reassure the children and calm them down before they would leave, but it seemed like the more she would try to comfort and reassure them the more they would cry. It was just heart breaking. She understood that as they got older and became involved in different things at school they would have less time to think about being apart from her. That was all good because, she reasoned, she didn't have a lot more time left on this side of the River. Having all three of her children in her life again and being able to watch her grandchildren grow up was all she wanted. Her life had now come full circle. She couldn't be happier. But, there is one sure thing; as long as you live life will always have one more curve ball to throw at you.

They had been settled in their new home for nearly a year. Late one evening Michael came home from work and began to check the day's mail. He was fully aware that the United States was in a war with North Viet Nam and the Viet Cong and that he, being in the Army Reserves, could be called up for duty at any given moment. He found a letter from his Army Reserves Headquarters. His outfit had been activated and he was ordered to report for duty. "O' Lord, not now, Please don't let it be!" he prayed. How could he tell his mother this? He had just got her comfortable and settled in their new home. She had just begun to live again. "Why now, Lord? Why now?" He had to pull himself together and break the news to his mother as gently as possible. He stayed in the den several minutes pondering this new situation, pacing the floor thinking about all the things he would have to do before he left but most of all he dreaded having to tell his mother this news. He wasn't sure how it would affect her. Finally he gathered himself, went to the bathroom, splashed cold water on his face and stood looking at his image in the mirror. "Here you go again, breaking your poor mother's heart. Will it ever end? Will you always be setting her up for a fall? Well, at least this time it's not your fault, it's not your idea to leave her; and this time, thank goodness, she won't have to wonder where you are she'll know where you are." This revelation made him feel a little better but he still dreaded having to tell her that he had to go away and might not come back alive – this time.

Lillie was sitting up in her bed watching a Christian Network Program. He could hear the gospel music as he approached the room. He peeked in and saw her feet patting in the air, her head nodding back and forth, enjoying herself. That made his task even harder ---- or, maybe not. She was in a Holy Ghost mode, a praise mode, so maybe it won't hit her so hard. He went into the room. "Hi, Mama." The song was ending, she looked up and happily greeted him.

"Hey, baby; I didn't hear you come in. How long you been standin' there watching me send up praises?"

"I've been in the house about 15 or 20 minutes I guess. I just came to your room, heard you enjoying yourself."

"Yes! I wuz having myself a shoutin' good time."

"Is your program over?" He was kind of hoping it was not over so he would have a few more minutes, but she quickly answered, "Yeah, they 's gone. It sho' wuz good, the Holy Spirit was in there, you could feel it. What you got on yo' mind, honey?"

He took a deep breath, sat down on the bed beside her, took her hand in his and trying to sound very 'matter-of-factly' he began.

"Mama, do you remember that I told you I had been in the army and when I got out of the army I joined the Army Reserves? Remember that?"

"Yeah, I 'member that," Her face began to frown, realizing that he must have some kind of bad news to tell her. She waited.

"Well, I got a letter today from Reserves Headquarters notifying me that my outfit has been activated because of the Viet Nam War."

"What that means?"

"Simply put, the army says they need me and I have to go."

"When you got to leave, tomorrow?"

He leaned over and kissed her on her cheek. "No, Sweetheart, I won't be leaving tomorrow. Guys with minor children or a dependent elder person like a mother or father will get two weeks to report, the others have one week. Because of your health and your age and the fact that you will be left all alone, by yourself, I believe they will give me two weeks. I'll need at least two weeks to get everything secured in the house, contact the bank, insurance companies and so forth. I know this will be hard for you ..."

"Now, no you don't! Don't you start to worrying 'bout me. You sound just like yo' daddy did years ago when he was goin' off to the war, mo' concerned 'bout me than yo'self. Child, you could lose yo' life but heah' you is 'round heah' worryin' 'bout how I'm gon' git along. Now, you just quit it, you hear me? I'll be just fine. You go ahead and do what you have to do and come on back home. It ain't like it was when you left home befo.' I know where you goin' this time and I know where to find you. I don't want you to leave me again but you have to do what the gov'ment say do. The Lawd' brought you back home to me once befo' and He gon' do it again, you watch and see."

"That's my girl! You know, you never cease to amaze me. Thank you for being so positive, Mama. It makes it a little bit ...not a lot, but a little bit easier to leave you." He got up from the bed, pacing back and forth, a very serious look on his face. "Now, first of all I am going to alert the family and the neighbors that I will be leaving. I know Tina will want you to come up there and stay with her. You can go if you want to, that may be the best thing for you." "Nope! I ain't goin' nowhere. I'm gon' stay right heah' in this house you bought for me. I'm a big girl; I can stay by myself. I ain't helpless. I can take care of myself, thank you!"

"Hold on, lady! I'm not telling you to do anything. You can do whatever you want to do. I just want you to be happy and well cared for, understand?"

"I"m gon' be happy right heah in my own house 'til you git back."

"OK, so that's done. Tomorrow I'll contact a Security Company and have an alarm system installed in the house. And I'll have a second credit card issued to you from my credit cards but I want you to be very careful, now; don't let nobody use them and don't give out no information from the cards over the phone; and don't let nobody know where -----, on second thought, I'll go to the bank and arrange a security setup for you. They'll know what to do. And, I'll ask David, Jr. and Jolita to make themselves available to drive you where you want to go. Can you think of anything else you might need? Tell me so I can take care of it before I leave."

Lillie couldn't think of anything. Mike had obviously given the matter a lot of thought before bringing it to his mother. In those minutes when he first read the letter, his mother's face and all she would have to endure without him here to help her came up before him like a panoramic movie screen. He knew some things would show up that he had not contemplated, he just wanted to be sure he had taken care of all the things he could take care of before he left. The next important thing he had to do was to let the family – David and the grandkids and Tina, know.

"I bet Tina's not home but I'll give her a try first and then try to get David." The phone rang and rang; just when the answering machine would've come on he hung up. "I'll try again later." He dialed David's number. "Hello, " it was Jolita.

"Hey, how's my favorite, most beautiful niece in the whole world?"

"Hi, Uncle Mike. You're the best, you know that?"

"Well, don't tell anybody else, let it be our secret, OK?"

"If you say so, but I'll tell the whole world, I don't care!"

They laughed, knowing they had a real mutual admiration. "Hey, Sweets, got a minute?"

"Sure, Uncle Mike, I always have a minute, even two, for my favorite uncle. What's up?"

"Now, listen carefully and ….. is your dad home, yet?"

"Not yet, he isn't. Can I give him a message for you, have him call you back?

"Yeah, you can tell him to call me but I still want to talk to you." He cleared his throat. " Sweetie, I just wanted to tell you that I'm gonna be going away for a while ….."

"Going away? Where? How come?!!"

"Calm down now, baby, let me explain. Remember I told you I was in the army once?"

"Yes, I remember. So?"

"Well, when I was discharged I joined the reserves and I got notice that my outfit has been activated to help in the Viet Nam War."

"What??!!!! Uncle Mike you must be kidding."

"No, no. I got the letter today and I have to report for duty in seven to 14 days. I am going to ask for 14 days so I'll have time to take care of everything Mama will need before I leave. That's what I want to talk to you and your dad about, and David, Jr., too." He could hear his niece sobbing. "Aw, baby, don't cry. I won't be gone forever, I'll be alright and I'll be back, don't worry, OK?"

"Why do *you* have go, Uncle Mike?"

"Because I am in the army and when the army calls I have to answer. I'm not the only one that's being called up, a lot of guys are being called. I'm not sure I understand what this Viet Nam War is all about; all I know is, the letter orders me to report to Reserve Headquarters so I have to go whether I want to or not. But I need you to do something for me while I'm away."

"I'll do anything, Uncle Mike."

"I need you to pay more attention to Mama while I'm gone. I want to know that you and David, Jr. will visit her more often than you visit now because I won't be around and she's gonna be missing me. I want you guys to try and fill in the void until I get back. Can you handle that?"

"Sure, that's not a problem. I'll sleep over with her and take her to the Malls, we'll have a blast! You don't have to worry, Uncle Mike, we'll take care of Granny. I know she's gonna miss you, I'm gonna miss you, too."

"Thanks, Sweetie, I knew I could depend on you"

"David, Jr., too. He loves Granny so much sometimes I think he could eat a piece of her." They laughed at it, but Michael understood what she meant. David, Jr. was Lillie's very first grand, so he was unique. He knew it, too. He also knew that his grandmother loved all of her grandchildren more than life and they were not jealous of one another.

"OK, babes, I've got to try and get to your Auntie Tina now. Tell your dad what we talked about and tell him he can call me if he wants to." Jolita sighed, sadness in her voice. "Alright, I'll tell him. Am I gonna see you before you leave?"

"Are you crazy, girl! I wouldn't leave without getting me some of that 'Brown Sugar of yours, I don't care what the army says! You got that?"

"I'm gonna miss you so much, Uncle Mike. You're the only uncle I've got!"

"And you're never gonna have another one. It's too late now, just ask Mama"

They laughed so loud you could hear them out doors!

"Uncle Mike, that's why I love you, you're such a nut!. But you're cool."

"Just remember that this 'nut' loves you and, by the way, you better not get married while I'm gone. I'll have to check out any guy that wants to marry you before you get hitched, you hear?"

"You don't have to worry about that, I'm gonna be like Auntie Tina, and not rush into any marriage."

"That's my girl. Be sweet, baby. We'll talk again soon."

He hung up the phone, seriously meditated for a minute or two about the deep bond of affection he and his nieces and nephews had formed since he came back home. Gosh! How he wished he had been here for their birth, see them learn to walk and talk. "O' well, thank God I'm here now." He dialed Tina's number, praying she would be home.

The phone rang two or three times, then, "Hey, there, Mama girl. What's up?"

"I"m *not* your mama, girl. Are you drunk or drinking?" Tina cracked up, laughing her head off.

"I saw the phone number on my Caller ID. I assumed it was Mama calling at this time of night, not you. I thought you would be out with your "squeeze" or out counseling or something," she giggled. "Well, you assumed wrong, silly woman. You know what they say about assuming. "

"No, I don't know what they say. What do they say?"

"To assume makes an ass out of u and me." Mike waited for her response.

"Yeah, right. Thanks for the info. Good to hear from you at any time, BMOC. What's up"?

"I got the news today that my Army Reserves Unit is being activated due to the Viet Nam War and I'm scheduled to report for duty in a week or two. I'm just letting everybody know since Mama will be in the house by herself. I want you all to take care of her until I get back."

"Boy! Life is always throwing her a curve. Dammit! It seems like just yesterday that you guys got back together and you're doing so well. She's happier than she's been in years. Why her? Why now?"

" She really amazed me, Tina. She's like a little girl that you found out she was more of a woman than you ever thought. She's not happy about me leaving her again, but she doesn't seem to be too concerned about it. I don't know, maybe she's said to herself, 'It's just another river I've got to cross, I'll cross this one the same way I crossed the other ones, trusting in God.' She's being a real trooper about the whole thing. "

"I'm glad to hear that. I know she doesn't want to come up here so what do you plan to do, put her in a nursing home like your sister-in-law wanted to do?", teasing him.

"If I didn't know you were joking, I'd put my religion aside for a minute and cuss your butt out, girl! She's already put her foot down about that. She told me flat out, 'I'm not leaving my house. I'm a big girl, I can take care of myself'.' "

Tina laughed. "That's my Mama! You go girl! So, what're you gonna do?"

"Well, I'm gonna try and make everything as secure and comfortable for her as possible. I'm having a Security System put in the house and Jolita promised that she and David, Jr. would come and sleep over often and spend more time with her so she won't be alone too much.. I'm also going to try and arrange with my bank to have an open account for her so all she has to do is order what she wants over the phone and have it delivered, charged to her account. I'm not comfortable with her having a credit card and being here alone. I think the bank will cooperate with me. And I know I can depend on you to keep in touch."

"Of course, that goes without saying. If there's anything else I can do, other than putting her into a straightjacket and bringing her up here with me, just let me know. "

Michael laughed at his sister's craziness. "I hope you won't have to go that far! I've alerted everybody that cares about her and I'm going to have all the protection that she will need in the house. So, I think she'll be OK."

"Did you let her stupid-ass daughter-in-law know?"

"Now, now, Sis, let's don't go there."

"I just wondered if she thought she would have to put up with Mama's bad English and 'terrible' diction again."

"O' no! Not if I can help it. Mama doesn't have to be anywhere that she's not wanted. She'll be OK. Look, I wish I could see you before I leave but there's not much time and I've got a lot to do. I'll call you again before I take off, though."

"OK, big guy, do what you have to do and if you think of anything that I can assist you in, you know you can call on me. Love you"

The army allowed Michael to take two weeks to get his mother settled but the time passed so quickly it seemed like only a day or two. He took care of everything he had in mind for her and was confident that she would be alright. Her faith in God would be the defining factor, however. Although he was devastated to have to leave his mother again, he believed that God would take care of both of them and bring them back together again. He had done it before and He would do it again.

> "You may feel down and feel like God
> has somehow forgotten;
> that you are faced with circumstances
> that you can't get thru.
> Right now it seems there's no way out,
> you're going under.
> God's proven time and time again
> He'll take care of you.
> He'll do it again;
> He'll do it again.
> Just take a look at where you are now,
> and where you been.
> Hasn't He always come thru' for you?
> He's the same now as then.
> You may not know how, you may not know when,
> But He'll do it again."

The day before Michael was to leave was a beautiful summer day. Unknowing to him the family had planned a surprise get-together. David and all the kids came and soon after that a van arrived and a couple men from a Catering Service began setting up a canapé, and picnic tables in the backyard; loading them up with all kinds of bar-be-cued ribs, chicken, hamburgers, hotdogs and everything imaginable for a cookout. Michael was so surprised! But the best was yet to come. By the time the caterers finished, a squeal of delight pierced the air. "Mickey" screamed, "Auntie Tina!"

Tina had flown in to be with the family, to say goodbye to Michael.

Al, her husband had business in LA and couldn't come with her but he had helped with the preparations via his office and hoped to join them before the day ended. That did not happen but he called that night; he and his brother-in-law had a long conversation. He promised Mike that he would always be there for his mother-in-law and pleaded with Mike not to leave home wondering and worrying about it. Al ended the conversation with, "Take good care of yourself, man. Love ya', see you soon." He was such a blessing to Tina and her family as well.

Needless to say, Lillie was overwhelmed! Her entire family was together in her presence again. Heaven couldn't be much better than this. Once more the awesomeness of God was made manifest in her life. Not only had He blessed her to have all three of her children with her, she was also blessed to have all her grandchildren there, as well - a third generation. There was such an outpouring of love between the little family. They were having so much fun and fellowship they hardly noticed the time. David finally told the gathering, "Well, guys, I'm afraid I'll have to take leave of all this fun. I've got early rounds in the morning."

Tina spoke up, "It's too bad that some of us have to work"

"Yeah, and the rest of us spend our time flying all over the world."

"Glad to be in that number," she laughed.

As if she had only just now noticed her absence, Lillie asked, "Where is Gloria? How come she didn't come wit' y'all?

"She had some kind of a Benefit Luncheon to attend. Knowing how long-winded those politicians are, they're probably still there."

"Before you go, honey, why don't you all gather 'round and let's pray. Michael, I want you to kneel right heah' in front o' me. The rest o' y'all join hands and make a circle 'round me and Mike." They all did as she told them. Taking her old and tattered Bible from what she called her "such-and-such- bag" that she kept hanging on the arm of her chair, she opened it to an already marked page and read:

> "Jabez was honorable above his brothers; but his mother
>
> named him Jabez [*sorrow maker*], saying, Because I bore
>
> him in pain.
>
> Jabez cried to the God of Israel, saying, Oh, that you
>
> would bless me and enlarge my border, and that Your
>
> Hand might be with me, and You would keep me from
>
> evil so it might not hurt me! And God granted his request."

"This is the prayer that I declare upon Michael. I want all o' y'all to agree wit' me cause Jesus said, 'Where two shall agree on earth as touching anything that they ask, it shall be done for them of My Father.' It ain't no doubt in my mind 'bout Michael coming back home safe and sound, but the devil is busy and he's all time trying to kill God's people. The way we defeat him is thru faith. Right now, in the Name o' Jesus, I plead the blood covering, the Precious Powerful Blood of Jesus, over Michael and I claim victory over any and all foes that may come against him. Everybody that agreed with that, say Amen."

A course of "Amen" came forth. It was done. "Now, I want ya'll to remember this day from heah' on; and every time you get together like we did today, I want you to remember to join hands and pray like we just did; cause it ain't nothin' but prayer and stayin' close to the Lawd thas' gon' get you through the world. So, don't forgit' to pray."

David departed, taking the two youngest children with him, but not before he hugged his brother and assured him, "Love ya' buddy. Don't worry, I'll be praying for you all the way. Just get this mess over with and hurry back to us."

"You bet, kid. Take care of yourself ... and Mama."

Lillie asked David, Jr. and Jolita, "Is y'all gon' leave, too?"

They didn't hesitate, "No, maam, we're spending the night with you and Uncle Mike."

"That's so sweet o' y'all" she told them, as Mike nodded his head in agreement.

"Well, I guess I'd better go inside and claim my territory, then," Tina said, looking at David, Jr. and Jolita, devilishly. The three of them jumped up and made a mad dash for the house. Michael yelled, "Hey you guys, don't tear Mama's house down in there!" Lillie leaned back in her chair, clapped her hands and roared laughing. "Tina is just as much a teenager as David, Jr. and Jolita. She ain't gon' never grow up." "I think you're right Mama. That girl is a riot."

Michael left the next day. Tina stayed over to accompany him to the airport. I suppose you could call his departure a "bitter-sweet" one for Lillie. This time his leaving left her with tears but they were different than the ones when he had left many years before. Her tears this time were for gratitude to God for what her son had become and for the love he had shown her since his return home.

This time he was not leaving rebelliously; he was leaving her in obedience to his country, and she was proud of him for that.

Over the next several weeks Michael called home as often as he could, checking on his mother and assuring her that he was fine and not to worry about him. Then one day, just as he had feared, his outfit was deployed to the Middle East. They would be in the thick of battle with the Viet Cong. When he called and told Lillie he would be going overseas, memories of when her husband Joe went overseas in World War I came flooding over her. It was like she was reliving her life. "Baby", she told him, "Don't you fear them 'Cong' folks. They cain't harm you 'cause you got the Blood o' Jesus covering you, and don't you forget it. David said in the Word of God, "A thousand may fall at your side and ten-thousand at your right hand, but it shall not come near you.' And I want you to rest assured that mama gon' be with you every minute of every hour of every day you're over there. I done told death he cain't have you 'cause you belong to God; so Satan can 'find a stump to fit his rump' and sit down somewhere, cause he can't have my baby!" Lillie had a way of speaking such faith, she could make the worst situations seem trivial, like child's play. Michael sure was thankful to have her on his side!

There was very little communication from Michael for a while. He did manage to send a couple of short – very short – letters and after that, nothing. Then after three months, which seemed more like three years, one day the doorbell rang and when Lillie answered, there stood two clean-cut, well-dressed servicemen, looking very serious. She knew they must be bringing bad news but it never even crossed her mind that her son was dead. She was confident that he could not be dead.

"Mrs. Lillie McClendon?" one of them asked.

"Yes, I'm her," Lillie told him. "What can I do for you?"

One of them gave their names, showing her their military identification; then one of them spoke up, "Maam, we regret very much to have to inform you that your son, Michael McClendon, is missing in action. His company was engaged in a heated battle several weeks ago and when it was over, he was not among the surviving members of his outfit. Search teams were dispatched to try and find him but to date all efforts have been futile. Since he could not be found, we can only assume that he has been captured by the enemy and is, more than likely, still alive. We just wanted to let you know that every effort has been made, and we will continue to make every effort to locate Sgt. McClendon. Rest assured, maam, we will not cease our efforts. We deliver these regrets of the President of the United States as well as the U. S. Army.

Lillie gave the young men a big "thank you" smile. "It sho' is sweet o' y'all to come and tell me. I know my son ain't dead, he's alive; if he wuzn't , the Holy Spirit woulda' done tol' me. He'll be alright and he's comin' back home, you'll see." The soldiers asked her if there was anything they could do for her. "No, no, son; thank you very much but I'm alright, I'm just fine. I'm sho' gon' tell Michael when he come home how nice ya'll is, heah?"

"Well, thank you very much, maam," one of them replied. We'll be on our way, now. It was very nice meeting you. We regret that our meeting had to be under such circumstances."

"That's alright, sweetheart. Like I said, my baby is alive. He'll be back."

The soldiers left and Lillie immediately got into her "praise" mode because, *"When praises go up, blessings come down."*

"I love to praise Him, (I love to praise His name)

I love to praise Him, (I love to praise His name)

I love to praise Him, (I love to praise Him)

I love to praise His Holy Name.

He's my Rock (He's my Rock)

My Rock, my Sword and Shield;

He's my Wheel, in the middle of a wheel;

He won't ever let me down,

He's just a jewel that I have found.

Hallelujah! Hallelujah!

I love to praise His Name

O' Hallelujah! Hallelujah!

I love to praise His Name.

Hallelujah! Hallelujah!

I love to praise His Holy Name.

Boy! You just should've seen Lillie in that house all by herself. Well, she wasn't really all by herself. The Holy Spirit was there and they were having themselves a hallelujah good time! Talking about praising the Lord! Lillie was doing it! "It's no wonder the Bible talks about David dancing all out of his clothes. When you get out of "self" and let the Holy Spirit take over, it's easy to dance out your clothes," she said. Anybody not knowing the Lord and not understanding how faith works would never understand what she was talking about. They would think she was crazy. You see, when *doubt* says, "It can't be done," *faith* says, "It's already done!"

Lillie remained in a praise mode for the next several days. Jolita and David, Jr., after she told them about Michael being missing, came over to stay with her. They tried to understand this attitude of hers. The son she loved so much is missing, no one knows where he is or whether he is alive or dead, and she is playing gospel records and shouting and just having a good old time! Still, they felt the need to be with her at this time. Weeks passed and no further word came about Michael.

David, Jr. and Jolita moved in with their grandmother, afraid to leave her alone. They talked to David about her, describing the way she was acting. He told them she was probably in denial, not willing to accept the fact that Michael was or could very well be dead. So the kids decided to move in with her so that she would never be alone, at least not at night. They loved her so much. They put almost all their extra curricular activities on hold so they would have more time to be with her. Not only did they love her, however, they enjoyed being with her, she was fun.

One Saturday night, Jolita had stayed home with Lillie while David, Jr. escorted his girlfriend to a dance. Lillie and Jolita were fast asleep when he came home, but his moving around from the kitchen to the living room looking for a snack and a late night movie awakened Lillie. She stood in the doorway, the old terrycloth robe she had worn for what seemed like 90 years, hanging drunkenly around her.

"Hey, baby; how long you been home?"

"Long enough to get into my pj's and make a sandwich. Did I wake you up"

"O' that's alright, honey. Did you have a good time out there where you went?"

"Yes, maam, it was nice." They talked for a few minutes. Then Lillie seemed to drift into a dream or something. She seemed to suddenly be in another world. David, Jr. didn't mention it to his grandmother, he just watched her with concern. All of a sudden, without looking at him, she told the boy, "Well, baby, I'm tired, I'm going back to bed. Come and give yo' best girl' some sugar."

She seemed to be struggling with a smile. That was so unlike her; she never had to make herself smile, she always had one ready. David, Jr. wondered about it but said nothing. He went over to her, helped her up, and then gave her a big hug and a kiss on her cheek. She seemed reluctant to let him go, holding him longer than usual. Finally she let go, squeezed his hand, and walked slowly to her bedroom.

The next morning, Jolita woke up to a strange eerie quietness. The usual smell of coffee was not there and there was no sound of Lillie watching the early news on TV. She instinctively headed to Lillie's bedroom. Lillie was still in bed. Jolita walked to the bed and softly called, "Granny." There was no answer or movement. Once more she called, louder this time, "Granny." Still no response and no movement. She leaned down and gently shook her grandmother, calling yet louder, "Granny!" Jolita was visibly nervous and concerned by this time. Something was wrong. She ran to David, Jr.'s bedroom. Trembling, her voice at an almost screaming pitch, "David! David, Jr.!"

He sat up in bed, rubbing his eyes. "What's the matter? What's wrong?"

Tears were ready to spill over in her eyes. "Something's wrong with Granny. She won't wake up, she won't say anything.!"

David sprang out of bed. It took about two long strides and he was standing beside Lillie's bed shaking her, calling frantically, "Granny! Granny! Granny!" Still no response and no movement. David, Jr. bent down close to her face to get a sense of her breathing. He could feel none. He began to panic. He knew something was indeed dreadfully wrong with his grandmother. He grabbed the phone and dialed his father's number. David, seeing his mother's name on his pager quickly answered.

"Good morning, Mama" assuming it was his mother calling. His son's hysterical voice answered.

"Dad, you got to come quick, something's wrong with Granny!.

"Dave, calm down, calm down and tell me what's going on.

David, Jr. was obviously terrified, irritated with his father's question. There was no time for a Q and A session, he wanted his dad, a physician, to get over there and take care of his grandmother! "Dad, she won't answer when we call her and she won't even move. She just lays there, not moving, not saying anything back to us. Dad, something is wrong with my Granny. You got to come quickly!"

"Dave! Dave! I want you to calm down and listen to me. I want you to call 911; identify yourself as my son. Tell them what you told me and tell them I said to get an ambulance to the house immediately. I am going to call Fred, her doctor, and alert him and then I'm on my way, OK? Do you understand?"

David, Jr. 's tears were flooding his face by now. He managed a tearful, "Yes, sir."

The young man followed his father's instructions.

The Medics, David and Lillie's doctor all arrived at the same time. David and Fred introduced and identified themselves to the medics and they all went into Lillie's bedroom. Fred examined her, searching for some sign of life. There was none. He took the stethoscope from his ears, turned to David and delivered the two small words that no one wants to hear about a loved one. "I'm sorry, she's gone." David stood there like a statute of stone. He looked at his friend as if he did not understand what he'd said. David was a physician but this was different, this was his mother he's talking about! Fred told the medics, "I'll be responsible for the death certificate. You can go ahead and do your job. David, you will have to tell them where to deliver the remains. "He put his arm around David's shoulder and guided him out of the bedroom. David, Jr. and Jolita were in the living room. One look at the faces of their father and Dr. Carter gave them the answer to the question they had been waiting for. Jolita sought the comfort of her father's arms but David, Jr. ran to Lillie's bedroom and hurling himself onto his grandmother's lifeless body, cried, "Granny! Granny! No! No! You can't leave me, Granny!" He cried hysterically. The medics allowed him a few minutes to vent his sorrow and then gently but firmly removed him to continue their work. Lillie's last words had been, "I'm tired..." She had at last given up. Hard trials and tribulations were now finished.

> *"On this Christian journey,*
>
> *my load gets hard to bear;*
>
> *I don't give up, I hold on fast,*
>
> *and kneel right down in prayer.*
>
> *But I get tired, my soul needs resting,*
>
> *Tired, my soul needs resting.*
>
> *I'm so tired, my soul needs resting;*
>
> *I can't stop now, it's where the saints*
>
> *have trod. I can't stop now it's where*

> *the saints have trod;*
> *No, I can't stop now*
> *It's where the saints have trod."*

Several months had passed and still there was no word from Michael. His outfit was contacted to notify him of his mother's passing but they said the search was still going on. They had not found his body and assumed that he had been captured. Her family was dismayed being unable to contact Michael but they had to do what they had to do. So David and Tina gave their mother a home-going that was fit for a queen. If Lillie could have given her opinion she probably would have said something like, "Baby, don't y'all do all that fo' me. I don' need all that. Just put one o' them pretty red roses on top o' my casket; that will be enough fo' me!" But she wasn't there to voice her opinion and this was the last thing in this world that they could do for her. It was going to be the best – and it was. White metallic casket covered completely with roses of every color – because she loved roses of all colors equally; a white carriage drawn by a beautiful white horse, the driver dressed in a white tux and white top-hat. The funeral cars were all white, the family dressed in white; and of course, Lillie was dressed in white. "Mama always said white is a symbol of purity. Wearing white for her home-going is a symbol of our pure love for her. If its one thing she taught us and lived it herself, it is *love*," Tina reminded the family. They placed a white marble headstone at the grave with the inscription:

God made the whole world
And then He made His Masterpiece;
Our Mother,
Mrs. Lillie McClendon

The Viet Nam War raged on. Michael's company was still overseas, still in the thick of the war. Very often they would send out reconnaissance missions; whose job was to search out and find enemies who were hiding in the brush and capture them or kill them. During one such mission, the patrol came upon what appeared to be a small village of Viet Cong people. They were able to surround the few straw huts and subdue the occupants without injuries or loss of life. They searched the huts for weapons, radios or anything that could be used against them. Apparently there were only women and children in the village, but the soldiers had to be sure. In one of the huts, lying on a bunk bed made of straw, was a tall very thin and bearded black man. His "dog tags" were still around his neck. The sergeant read the inscription on the tags: "Michael J. McClendon, Master Sergeant, U.S. Army." The man slowly opened his eyes. It was obvious that he was very weak but they could see no signs of any injury. Seeing the figures standing there, he weakly moaned, "Ma---ma; Ma---ma." They looked at each other then told him , "Sergeant, we've been looking for you. It's good to see you;" which he totally ignored, only staring at the men. "Ma—ma" he spoke again, seemingly trying to understand why "she" wasn't responding to him. The men decided that it was delirium and opted not to ask him any questions. He was wearing dog tags that identified him as a Master Sergeant in the U. S. Army and that was enough for them. They placed him on a makeshift cot and carried him back to their camp. The commanding officer called for a helicopter to come and take Michael to a hospital in Japan. He was there for more than four months receiving treatment for extreme undernourishment, dehydration, kidney and liver problems as well as psychological problems. For the longest time, he addressed everybody as "Mama" whether they were male or female. Many interrogations revealed that he had been rendered unconscious by a grenade blast during fierce fighting. Most of the guys in his patrol had either been killed or seriously wounded in the fighting but he was thrown several yards away from them, not seriously wounded but he was out of plain view, hidden by thick underbrush until some village people – Viet Cong – found him. They were supposed to be the enemy but they took him to their village, kept him out of sight and gave him what little care they were able to give him keeping him alive until he was found.

Having been told of the death of his mother, the army notified David that Michael had been found and was in a hospital in Japan. Since David was a physician the army doctors were happy to collaborate with him in an effort to give Michael the help he needed. David gave them the history of his mother's and Mike's relationship, how they had been separated for years then reunited and became very close before he was called back into the service. They decided that for the time being it would be unwise to tell him of his mother's death. When he was well enough he was sent to a hospital in the states where he received intensive physiological care for another six weeks.

The day finally arrived when he was released from the hospital and given a 30-days furlough. At last he was going home to see his Mama. Arriving at the train station an hour early he decided to take a walk. It wasn't long before a small flower shop caught his eye. This was wonderful! He could take his mother some of her favorites – roses. He thought, "At least I can take her flowers since I have not been able to get out and shop for a nice gift for her. He walked over to the shop, surveyed the flowers on hand. Deciding on roses, he asked what the cost of a dozen roses would be. The shop owner asked him how far he would be traveling. "All day today, all night tonight and arrive around 4 o'clock tomorrow afternoon."

"If you're gonna be riding that long, as hot as it is, I wouldn't advise you to spend a lot of money on flowers because they'll be all wilted and dying or dead by the time you get where you're going."

"I understand what you're saying but, you see, my mother loves roses and she would be thrilled to get some roses, they're her favorites."

"O, I see. I only have two or three decent looking roses." He showed Mike three roses. "See, they're already starting to wilt and since you won't have any water to put them in …. Well, it's up to you, son, if you want them you can have them free of charge. My treat."

"Well, that sure is nice of you, sir, but I don't mind paying for them."

"No, no; like I said, it's my treat. That's the least I can do for you fellas who're risking your life in this stupid war. Be my guest, take the roses." Mike was impressed.

"Well, thank you very much. I'll take the three."

To him it seemed like forever, but before long he found himself getting off the train, back home again. He flagged a taxi and with some help from the driver threw his bags into the car. He gave the driver the address while surveying the city. It had changed even in the short time he had been gone. He soon found himself in front of the house he and his mother had shared. It looked alone, empty, for some reason. He paid the driver then slowly walked onto the small porch. He rang the doorbell, there was no answer. He rang again, still no answer. Perhaps David, Jr. or Jolita had taken his mother shopping or something. Soon he realized no one was inside the house and took a seat in the little porch swing he had bought for Lillie to sit and watch the kids play.

"Hey young man," a voice called. "Are you Michael?" It was the man who lived across the street.

"Yes sir, I'm Michael"

They exchanged greetings, then he asked Michael, "Have you talked to your brother or any of your family, yet?" That struck Michael as kind of strange but he answered, "No sir, not yet. I wanted to see Mama, first."

"Then maybe you need to call your brother."

I went to the house where I used to live.

The grass had grown up and covered the door.

Someone across the street

asked me "who do you seek?"

"For no one lives there anymore."

Then I went to the church

where I used to go.

The preacher was still there,

and met me at the door.

He said, "I know who you are,

and I know who you're looking for,

But they don't come here anymore."

"They are somewhere around the

throne of God. They are somewhere

around the throne of God."

> *I'll keep searching, and searching,*
>
> *until I find them. They are somewhere*
>
> *around the throne.*

Michael got a tremendous feeling of foreboding; a feeling like he was not going to like what his brother would have to say. For sure, David hadn't gone through with the plan he had once before to put their mother in a nursing home. God forbid! "Come on over to my house and you can use the phone," the man invited him.

Michael followed the man. He went into the house and rang David's phone in his office. "Mike! Where are you? "

"I'm at a neighbor's house across the street from Mama's house."

"You're in town? You're home?"

"Yes, I'm home."

"Stay right there, I'm on my way."

David flew out of his office, jumped in his car and sped to his mother's house. How wonderful to see his brother again! It was truly a miracle. For a while they did not know whether they would ever see him alive again. Lillie said she had pleaded the Blood of Jesus over Michael and rebuked death. She knew what she was talking about! These thoughts came into David's mind as he hurried to see his brother. Once he arrived, David and Michael hugged each, slapping each on the back and crying. They were two happy young men! When they finally released each other, Michael asked the question that David knew was coming and the one that he would pay a million dollars not to have to answer. "Where is Mama?" The psychologists in the army hospital had told David how he should break the news of his mother's death to Michael. So David began the long tedious task of telling his brother that his mother had passed away and the circumstances surrounding her death. Nothing he could say, as he well knew, could soften the blow. It was done, it was God's choice, and no one could argue with His will. As though Lillie was there comforting him – she *was* there in spirit – Michael looked up toward the sky and mumbled, "Lord, I sure do thank You for taking her home the way You did; no long illness and no suffering. You let her just sleep away, and for that I am so grateful. You didn't even let her have to go through the worry of what happened to me. I thank You for that, also, because she was too old to have to go through that, worrying about me --- again!. God is such a Good God!" David shook his head in agreement. "Yes, He is."

"Where did you bury her? I want to go to the cemetery."

David checked his watch. "I'm not sure the superintendent is still there; it's almost six o'clock now, they lock the gates at exactly 6. But we can give it a try and if it's closed we can go in the morning. Where're your bags? Let's get them into the car."

"They're over on Mama's porch."

They thanked the neighbor and walked across the street to Mama's house.

"What happened to the house, is it in foreclosure? It looks empty."

"No, it's not in foreclosure! We've kept it secured, locked up, waiting to hear from you. In fact, David, Jr. and Jolita both have keys to the house and the electricity and water are still on because from time to time the kids come over and mow the lawn and dust the house inside, etc., trying to keep it looking good for your homecoming. You know how those two are about you and Mama."

Michael smiled. "Yes, I love them, too, more than they'll ever know. "

They called Tina, luckily she was in New York, and so she grabbed a plane right away and flew down to be with her brothers. Lillie's three children were together again.

In the morning the three of them went to the cemetery. Michael still clutched one of the roses he had brought with him, the only one that had survived the heat. Just as the storeowner predicted they had wilted and faded from the heat. Yet he held on to one of them. When they reached Lillie's grave Michael read the inscription on the beautiful white marble headstone, and a thousand memories of his mother flooded over him. He remembered his youth and how if it had not been for his mother's prayers and steadfast faith in God, he would have lost his life while he was still a very young man; how she did not stop praying for him and her effectual fervent prayers saved him and turned his life around; how, when he had to go fight in the Viet Nam War, she laid hands on him, prayed the Prayer of Jabez and claimed the covering of the Blood of Jesus for his safe return; how he was miraculously saved from a blast that should have killed him but instead, it threw him out of harm's way; how the Lord used Vietnamese people who should have been his enemies and turned them into angels to nurse him and keep him alive until the army could find him. During his worse times, in his afflictions, his mother's face was always before him. At the end he could hear her say, "My baby gon' be alright, I don't need to pray for him no more; so I'm goin' home and be wit' my Father." That's when all the cares of this life fell away and she happily walked into the outstretched arms of her Savior Jesus Christ.

Tina and David watched through tear-blinded eyes as Michael knelt beside his mother's grave mixing tears with the petals from the faded rose as he slowly pulled them out and dropped them one by one onto her grave.

Petals from this faded rose,

is all I have to give;

But, Mama, I tried to make you happy,

while you lived.

If I had a million dollars,

I'd line your grave with gold;

but that wouldn't wake you

from your sleep,

while eternal ages roll.

So petals from this faded rose, Mama,

is all I have to give.

But Mama I tried to make you happy,

while you lived.

****

But without *faith* it is impossible to please and be satisfactory to Him.. For whoever would come to God must [necessarily] believe that God exists and that He is the rewarder of those who earnestly and diligently seek Him [out].
(Hebrews 11:6; Amp. Bible)

ISBN 141208917-4